RULES AND ROSES

Pookie Sho

DEDICATION:

To my mother Gladys Miranda, this is for you!

To

Des Massalay

You know the

LOVE is DEEP +

Love,

Pookie Sho

I

"I often think that the night is more alive and more richly coloured than the day" – Vincent Van Gogh

The night was her playground! It was an array of both the good and the bad. Evening tea sellers had come out with their display of beverages, eggs and bread, ready to sell to the hungry night walkers. Bars played loud afro pop music filled with drunken men flirting with the waitresses and any lady that tickled their fancy. The roads were awfully busy as bus conductors called out for passengers and the pickpockets roamed around, eyes like hawk waiting to pounce on their prey. Then there was her, the night queen! At night, she could bask in the self-reflected glow of her own pleasure! Leya called herself the queen of the night, she owned it and made it dance to her tune. After all, she was an extremely gorgeous slender young lady with a sculpted figure, an hour glass shape that made men lust after her. She had sexy plump lips, perfectly shaped eyebrows looking down on her long natural eyelashes and glossy skin - her beautiful caramel skin tone was to die for! Besides, this was Lagos and image was everything! As she walked towards the Point hotel, she pondered. Who would have thought that someday she also, would get to see the interior of the best rated luxurious hotels in Lagos? A place where the creme de la creme of society gathered to do business or simply relax. Her head high, amidst the stares and cat calls from bus drivers and passers-by, she gyrated her hips provocatively, smiling confidently and occasionally pulling down her mini skirt that kept riding high up her thighs, revealing her red lace underpants. As she got closer to the hotel, she reached into her cross body bag hanging down her right shoulder to bring out her phone. Dialling a number, she put the phone to her ear as it rang. Just as she approached the revolving doors, the hotel guard, a man in his mid-forties, stout with a large protruded belly that caused his shirt buttons to pop open, blocked her way with his hands wide open, almost aggressively. He looked her up and down in sheer disgust and in the commonly spoken pidgin language asked, "Madam, where you dey go?" "What do you mean where I dey go" she retorted, trying to shove him aside as she put her phone back in her bag. The guard firmly stood his ground, unflinching as he continued to block her way. "I said where you dey go?" He asked again, his eyes moving from her sheer cropped, thin strap black top that revealed her bra down to her dogtooth mini skirt and red stiletto. "I am here to see a friend so will you put your stupid hands down and let me pass" Leya angrily tried to push her way through. *How dare he?* She thought. Did he not know who she was? The queen! The night belonged to her - no one challenged the queen!

The guard moved towards the direction she tried to make a pass for, and responded in a sarcastic tone, "Friend abi? We know una type. You wan carry ashawo enter this kind hotel shey? It won't happen," he nodded his head in a frown. "My friend, will you get out of my way you idiot" grabbing his arm and trying to push him aside. Still defiant, he responded, "Ehnnn, I like it. Idiot o, foolish o, you no go enter. Call your friend make he come meet you for outside. This no be chop and go hotel." She looked at him for a moment as he rolled his eyes at her and looked in the other direction, arms still wide open. Kissing her teeth at him, Leya reached into her bag to get her phone out again. She dialled the number, and as it rang through, she began to pace up and down appearing frustrated at the lack of response. The hotel guard stared at her and burst into laughter. Turning to him briefly with angry eyes that could pierce the soul, she continued to dial the number.

****

"Alright Mr Daniels, have your people call my people" the older grey haired man said as he shook hands with Jay Daniels at the entrance of the Point hotel. Jay was a young man in his early thirties with a visible scar under his right eye and a dapper patchy beard style – the hair much thicker on his chin and his moustache a stubble length that gave him an appealing wild look. "Sure thing, Mr Silva" Jay acknowledged. Watching Mr Silva walk away to his car, his attention was drawn to the loud noise and squabble between Leya and the hotel guard. This was unusual, as the Point hotel was not known for such spectacle. Curiously, Jay walked towards them with a slight frown on his face just as Leya turned to walk towards him. She brushed past aggressively, pushing him off balance whilst still hurling insults at the security guard. Gathering his composure, he turned to look at Leya walking away angrily. He noticed her tattoo – stars in a vertical line from the nape of her neck down her back. Jay called out to her, "Excuse me, are you okay? Lady! Lady?" she turned to him in anger and snapped, "WHAT!" Calming herself down, she proceeded to respond in a more sober tone. "Sorry, what? I'm not......" He cut in, "Are you okay?" "No! No, I'm not okay, okay?" she responded, getting agitated again. "I am here to meet a friend and that idiot," pointing towards the direction of the front guard who was back at his post greeting guests arriving at the hotel all smiles like nothing had happened. "The idiot would not let me in, calling me all sorts and telling me I cannot enter dressed like this. I mean, look at me" she said, gesturing at her body and turning around arms open. "What is wrong with what I'm wearing?" He looked at her face briefly, thinking what a beautiful girl she was and then down her body to check out the outfit. He hesitated for a second and then said "Ermmm, some hotels have a strict code on who goes in and out. I mean, this..." he gestured to her outfit, "...might come across a bit unconventional and give off a not so good statement." Jay looked over at the front guard, then at Leya, and with authority he said to her, "Come with me" as he walked back towards the front guard. Leya frowned at his command but she followed obediently. "Bayo," he called out to the front guard. Bayo's steps quickened, walking hurriedly towards Jay and bowing in respect. "Mr Daniels, good evening sir." He said, adjusting his shirt and ensuring it was well tucked in. "Good evening" Jay responded. "This lady here says you refused her entry." Bayo looked at Leya with the same look of disgust he gave earlier and confidently said, "Oga, na dem!" Jay looked at him confused "Sorry, na who?" He asked, abruptly turning to Leya and back to Bayo who raised his hands, placing them on his head. "Hah! Mr Daniels, these girls are dangerous o. They will wear small, smallllllll cloth" stressing his words, "and come and say they are looking for their friend. Which friend? Her friend is not here o, she should go and look for where she kept that friend" he said looking at Leya. Leya interjected angrily, "It's not your fault you morbid dog, if..." "Mr Daniels, you see?" Bayo interrupted her, his palm and fingers pointing at Leya as the two began an exchange of words. Jay, exasperated, raised his hands to try and stop Leya who in anger had taken off one of her heels to hit Bayo. "Hey, that's enough!"

Jay shouted, startling both of them who stopped to look at him. Bayo bowed in an apologetic manner "Sorry sir." "Okay," he said to Bayo, "Just go back to your post, I'll handle this." Watching as Bayo reluctantly walked back to his post, Jay turned to Leya, "Now you, I don't know which friend you are here to see but....." Leya interrupted him angrily "Don't you, you me! Ah ah, which one is now you? I said I am here to see someone, I cannot get through to his number but he is lodged here" she continued. Jay sighed! "Okay, walk in with me" He mentioned to her as Leya caught a sniff of his cologne. The whiff lingered all over, exuding some sort of masculinity she found alluring. *He looked like one of those men who graced the covers of that magazine, what was the name again?* She thought to herself. *"Ahh, GQ model"* she smiled in her thoughts. Jay walked towards the revolving doors with her behind. Leya turned to see Bayo staring at her angrily in defeat as she followed Jay into the hotel. Sticking her tongue out at him, she chuckled.

The hotel interior was everything Leya ever imagined. All marbled floor, amazing decor that made one feel like they had just walked into a show room filled with all types of luxurious furniture and accessories. The lobby screamed class! She looked around in awe, transported into one of her many day dreams. As the contemporary sophisticated chandeliers hung on the high ceiling, with every single cushion pillow complimenting the seats they lay on and guests being treated with the utmost respect and professionalism, Leya imagined she was one of the hotel guests. The atmosphere was idyllic, the hotel staff went about their duties and bowed in salutation to their guests as they walked by.

Jay walked to the front desk and the receptionist's face lit up in a shy almost embarrassed way, her man crush forever! "Good evening Mr Daniels" she greeted with a smile. "Good evening Tola" he responded smiling back. *"Maybe one day"* Tola thought, as she composed herself. "Any messages since I've been in the meeting?" Jay asked, turning briefly to look at Leya who was completely lost in her own world. He was intrigued by her. Who was she? Who was this guest she was here to meet? Man, Woman? He was jolted back to the present when he heard Tola mention, "Yes sir, your mum called and asked for a call back as soon as you can" He nodded in acknowledgment. Leya propped her elbow on the front desk looking at Jay and Tola confused. *"Why would his mother call him at a hotel?"* Leya thought. She turned around still in awe at the hotel interior. "Any more?" Jay asked. "Oh yes sir, Mr Chike brought in the proposal." His face brightened up in a suppressed smile, "Ahhh, yes. Where is it?" He asked Tola who appeared to be going through his messages on the computer screen. "Miss Beverley took it up to your suite sir." She said, looking up at him. "Thank you" he responded, smiling at Tola who smiled back blushing. "*Yes, one day. Just one day*" she thought to herself, admiring the 6ft 4inches of absolute deliciousness called Mr Daniels whose titan shoulders swayed as he walked with athletic gait towards the elevator. Tola's attention drew to Leya who was walking quickly to catch up with Jay. "Can a skirt be any shorter? Very lucky she's with the boss" Tola murmured. "Are you the manager?" Leya asked as they got to the elevator. He turned to look at her as he pressed the elevator button, simultaneously looking at his watch. "No, why?" He asked. "Welllll" Leya responded, "Everyone seems to know you. Or you must be one of those returning guests who stay at the same hotel each time they are in town. Your mum called? You're one of those mummy's boy abi?" smiling coyly at him. The elevator doors opened and a lady walked towards them smiling at Jay in obvious recognition. "Heyyy" she said sheepishly. "Ify, hiiii" Jay responded surprised to see her, as they both attempted an awkward hug. "Fancy meeting you here," he said to her. "I know, been what? Ages" she replied. "So, what brings you here?" he asked. "You know, work and all. Here to meet a client who just bought a property in the country and looking for some ideas" she said, playing with her hair, all flustered like a school girl who had just met her crush. "I see..., we should catch up sometime" Jay replied. "I'd like that" she responded almost flirtatiously. "You have my number right?" She enquired. "Yeah, I'll call you" He smiled. "Looking forward to that" Ify smiled back as they gave each other another hug, this time more relaxed. Leya looked at both of them suspiciously and then at Ify who walked away sizing Leya up. Her gaze particularly focused on Leya's outfit. "See?" Leya said, lightly tugging at Jay's arm to grab his attention, "I'm not the only one here to meet somebody." Jay turned to look at her whilst waiting for the elevator to open again. "Who is she anyway? And why was she acting funny?" She asked. "Funny?" Jay asked. "Ehen now, she was just putting imaginary hair behind her ear and behaving like a babe who had just met the man she likes" Leya replied, Jay chuckled! The elevator opened and they got in, "You're very inquisitive. By the way, has your friend not......" her phone began to ring and she muttered in anger, "Speak of the devil." Jay scrolled through his phone as Leya picked her call. "What kind of rubbish is this now? I have been here all evening, on top all kinds of insult and embarrassment just..........Your wife??" Leya shouted, drawing Jay's attention to her. "So you wanted me to come and meet you when your wife was around? D..dd..ddont annoy me" she stuttered in anger. "Because of you, I had to buy a new outfit, I am still owing the stupid girl 3k sef! Fixed my hair, did my nails o, now called Uber alllllll the way" gesturing with her hands and almost poking Jay in the eye. She looked at him and whispered "Sorry." Jay stole glances at her, smiling at her conversation, all the while pretending to be busy on his phone. "I am so dressed to kill ehnn. How many opportunities would I get to come to the Point Hotel?" Leya continued, still yelling at the caller. Jay looked at her briefly, then at her "dressed to kill" outfit and slightly nodded his head in amusement. "I came here to meet you and you are now mentioning wife." The elevator door opened and Jay gestured with his hand in courtesy for Leya to step out before he did. She stepped out totally ignoring him and continued her conversation as they began to walk down the corridor. "Where are you sef? I am here wai............ehnnnnn!!! She exclaimed, her eyes wide opened, as she took a look at her phone briefly before putting it back to her ear. "You said what?? Hah, my God will punish you, my God will punish you. You will shit seven days straight, idiot. May thunder locate you wherever you are and strike you down" she hung up! Jay stopped to look at her thinking how feisty she was, yet so appealing. "Can you imagine?" She asked Jay who nodded at her confused and responded with a "No." She began to pace up and down the corridor. "Calm down" he said. "Calm down? Did you say calm down? I was there minding my business o, eating my suya and drinking my sprite with my friend. That was how the idiot came to our table, started a conversation, he said he liked me and would I like to have dinner with him? You know now, as per getting to know each other" Leya tried to explain to Jay who continued to stare at her, more interested in knowing who this feisty, gorgeous, 5ft 5 girl was. How come he had never seen her anywhere prior to this night? She probably worked in an office on the mainland, he thought. He heard a voice continue, "He now told me he is here on business and was staying at the Point hotel. I heard Point hotel, I said ahhhhh big boy. Let me arrange myself well. He asked what I was doing tonight, I said I'll be working." "Working?" Jay interrupted. "Yes now, working" Leya answered as she continued her rambling. "He said okay, I should try and come and see him bla bla bla. Can you imagine the idiot is actually a mechanic around my area? Mechanic in that jungle where I live. Telling me about his 7 children, 7!!!" She exclaimed, raising her fingers to Jay who had now propped his body against the door of his suite looking at her in sheer amazement. "Hah, Leya! LEYA! You have suffered in this life. So it is me someone has just 419'd like that?" She asked looking at Jay. "Me!" She mentioned again. He shrugged his shoulder and began to speak, "Well....." She interrupted him. "See as he has just wasted my time. Time is money mehnn." She caught Jay smiling. "What's funny?" "Technically, you played yourself" he replied her. "What do you mean?" she asked, an irritated look on her face. "You meet a man in..." "My area" she answered. "So, this man obviously tells you things you wanted to hear and you jumped at it." "Well......" Leya said pondering, unable to answer the question. "Well?" Jay asked, waiting for her response. "I don't know! Look, I have to go." She turned to leave, "Wait" he called after her, she turned. "It's very late. There are predators out there.

13

I mean, why don't you stay and then leave in the morning." Jay offered. "Leave where in which morning? Did you not hear my time is money? I still have a lot of hours and can make up for the time wasted." Jay looked puzzled, "Where do you work?" he asked, slotting his door card and slightly opening the door. She paused for a few seconds and blurted out, "Body shop." "Body shop? Oh, like a massage parlour" as he beckoned Leya to enter the suite. She peeped into the room before she entered, looking around in awe. He caught her gaze and smiled before saying, "So body shop right?" She nodded in silence, oblivious to Jay or his conversation. She was fascinated by the sheer beauty of the room. His hotel room was bigger than the house she lived in. She felt like she had just walked into one of those mansions she saw in her favourite telenovela series. A 50 inch flat screen television hung on the wall, the bed was king size with white Egyptian cotton sheets. The room had a leather sofa, its own desk and chair. On the other end of the room, she could see the open terrace overlooking the blue sea and a transparent glass door with a Jacuzzi that could house 5 people at a go. "Wow!" she whispered in delight. He smiled at her sudden innocence, almost like a little girl in a Barbie shop! "So, how about I ask you to be my masseuse tonight and I pay you. It's been a long day and I could do with a massage" he said rubbing his neck. "How much do you charge?" Leya jolted back to reality! Turning to him, she began counting and marking her fingers one after the other blurting out, "I don't give head, I don't do threesomes, don't touch my vagina, just do your thing and finish, I don't kiss on the lips, no kinky rubbish, no golden showers and don't come and be pressing my breast like you want to bake bread." Jay looked on at her in utter shock as she continued to speak unaware of the look on his face. "I charge by the hour and after one round, price is double. I take cash mostly but only card? Don't worry, I have POS" bringing out a point of sale machine from her bag and showing it to Jay who was as speechless as a stone! "Now" she continued, bringing out packs of condoms and showing them to him, "Which one do you like?" "You're a call girl?" He asked, finding his speech. Leya suddenly turned uncomfortable at the realisation he had not been aware all the while. She clutched the condoms in her hands and said quietly, "You asked how much I charged?" "No, nooo" Jay responded, rubbing his beard confused. "I asked how much a massage cost when you said you worked at the Body Sh......." like a light bulb moment, it hit him! "Body shop!" He laughed. "Now I get it." "Are you still interested or should I leave?" Leya asked, her face straight. "No! No don't leave" Jay exclaimed. "Not sure how I've managed to end up with a call girl in my suite but, how about we start with introductions." "Introductions?" Leya asked puzzled. "Yes, like names first." "Oga, no time for all this now. Ah! Okay, my name is Leya" she mentioned. "Real name or alias?" he asked smiling coyly. "Real.....well, I gave myself that name and everyone knows me as Leya." "So, what's your real name?" he asked. "I don't want to talk about that" she replied in a standoffish manner, moving to put the condoms back in her bag. "So, are you ready?" She asked again, walking towards him. "Ready? You haven't even asked my name." She put her hands on his belt and whispered in his ear, "You can tell me later." He could smell her cheap perfume which swirled around him, almost nauseating. Gathering himself, he pushed her back slightly. "I'm only in the mood for company tonight, nothing else. Tell you what? How about that massage and I pay?" She looked at him almost confused, noticing his almond shaped eyes with the scar underneath, angular cheekbones sculpted down his jaw and well chiselled body. Leya had met a lot of men in her life but this man standing before her was a delight to look at. "Only massage" She said to him, he nodded. "How much?" He asked, his face serious. She stared at him and smiled sheepishly, "Massage is very expensive o, I have to be using all my power to rub your body." "How much?" He asked again looking at her intensely, his gaze penetrating her body. "Errmmm" she turned around to assess the room. Thinking of a price, she blurted, "30k!" "30 thousand naira? Hmm, okay then. Say I double that and have you till morning?" he asked. For some odd reason, Jay did not want her out on the streets and this was an offer he knew a call girl would not resist. Leya's face turned into shock, mouth opened. This was not what she was expecting when she set out to the Point hotel. At least, maybe eight thousand naira after show. And yet, this man was offering her sixty? *Sixty for nothing but a massage? She thought* "Yessss?" he reiterated, waiting for her response. She nodded in shock approval. "C-c-can I make a quick call?" She stuttered - her weakness when she was nervous. "Sure" Jay replied, walking towards the walk in wardrobe next to the area where the Jacuzzi was, unbuttoning his shirt. Leya hurriedly rushed to the bathroom, removed her phone from her bag and dialled a number.

2

"Free yourself from expectations. The best will come when and from where you least expect it" – Anonymous

She had known from the moment she met Bunmi, that this was the big sister she never had. Bunmi was bubbly, personable, very loud and brash, quick tempered and protector of all things Leya. She had worked the streets long before Leya and knew the ins and out of the trade like the back of her hand. The other girls feared her and she liked that sense of authority as the Mother hen!

Leya put the phone to her ear as it rang. Bunmi picked up! "Hello? Hello Bunmi" she tried to whisper looking towards the door, checking to make sure her new client was not eavesdropping on her call. "Leya baaaabyyyy. Ah ah, how far now? Wetin big boy dey talk?" Bunmi responded excitedly. "Which big boy? Abeg forget that one, I'll give you gist when I come back" Leya answered. "Ah ah, wetin happen?" Bunmi asked concerned. "Bunmi! Bunnnmiii" she stressed, "If you see the big fish wey….." Leya had not finished her sentence when she heard Bunmi already in a fight with one of the girls who lived in the same compound. "Ashawo! Your mama. Oya try it now, trrryyy it, let me show you pepper." Leya shook her head at the all too familiar situation. "Hah! Bunmi you're not even listening to me." Leya said. "No vex jare baby girl, no be that Charity girl wey get leg like chewing stick who come dey look for my trouble?" Bunmi responded, Leya laughed. "You and these girl sef. Any way you can sha handle her. Ehen, as I was saying……." Jay interrupted with a knock on the door "Leya, food is here." "Oh! Okay, coming right out" she answered. Bunmi broke down in laughter teasing Leya, "Ah ah, coming right out! See as your English just polish now now! Coming right out. No be small coming……." Leya interrupted her giggling, "Abeg, abeg. Let me give you correct gist tomorrow." "Tomorrow keh? You dey stay all night ni?" Bunmi asked. "Yep!" Leya responded confidently, "and he is paying me sixty cool k." Bunmi exclaimed in shock,

"Sixty what? Blood of Jesus! Hah! Sixty k" she shouted. Charity, clearly irritated by Bunmi's conversation, looked at her angrily, "Why are you shouting like a mad woman?" Bunmi turned to her, her blood boiling, "Mad woman abi? Let me show you mad woman." Bunmi yanked her wig off and charged towards Charity, landing a hard punch on her face. Leya whispered amidst the commotion, "Oya fight o, me I'm going." Bunmi's phone still by her ear and supported by her left shoulder, continued to rain hard punches with her fist on Charity's face. The other girls tried to intervene, pulling her away. Leya smiled, shaking her head at the loud fight going on over the phone and hung up.

She walked back into the room to see Jay in a more informal outfit. His black vest sat so well on his broad chest, a true reflection of his build and the loose grey joggers enhanced his already long legs. "Not sure what you wanted to eat so I got the guys to bring a variety" he said to her sitting down and picking up the TV remote. Leya opened the dishes on the cart and could not believe how much food there was. "But who is coming to eat all these food?" she asked surprised. "How can you eat all this and still be able to jangalova?" Jay laughed, "Janga what?" He asked.

She popped a spoonful of the baked Alaska dessert in her mouth and responded to Jay with the spoon still in her mouth "Jangalova now, jiggy jiggy!" He laughed again, "Where do you get these words from? First you wished for thunder to strike someone, then you hoped he had a bad toilet experience...." Leya put another spoonful of dessert in her mouth. *"This thing is nice o"* she thought to herself before interrupting Jay. "You're not street at all. Mummy's boy" she teased him smiling. Suddenly, he tapped on to the sit next to him beckoning her to come sit down. She put her spoon down and moved towards him, her skirt riding high up again as she tried to pull it down. He noticed her action and asked, "You want something more comfortable?" She nodded. Jay got up and walked towards his closet, returning a few moments later with one of his t shirts.

"W-w-what was your name again? She asked in an initial stutter as she toyed with the shirt in her hands nervously. He giggled, "I don't remember you stammering all evening so what's with the stutter?" She became quiet and overwhelmed with a sudden wave of shyness. Leya! Shy? Where did this come from? Jay, sensing her nervousness, looked at her smiling, "I never told you my name but now you've asked, my name is Jason Daniels but everyone calls me Jay." She stared at him for a second, stretching her hand to shake his, "Nice to meet you" she said, a pretend serious look on her face. Jay chuckled at the gesture and responded, "Nice to meet you too." The room was filled with a moment of silence, the atmosphere tense as they stood staring at each other, their hands still in a warm shake. Suddenly Leya blurted out, "Can we start?" This startled Jay as he laughed, tilting his head back. "I told you, I am only in the mood for company tonight." He stared at her for what felt like forever. His eyes! Despite the scar which she was curious about, there was something about his eyes that looked deep into one's soul. Those almond shaped, beautiful light brown eyes were almost sexual that she felt his gaze could undress her. "I, I need to change" Leya blurted out again, hurriedly walking away into the bathroom. Closing the door behind her, she propped herself at the back breathing heavily. Walking towards the mirror, she looked at her reflection, "Leya what is wrong with you? This is business! Get yourself together abeg" she reminded herself, slapping her face. Moments later, she changed into his t-shirt and walked out.

She walked into the room, Jay's t shirt clearly oversized, hanging on her beautiful frame. Sitting on the leather sofa watching a show on TV, remote in one hand and a drink in the other, his eyes turned to look at her and stared for a moment. His t-shirt may have been oversized but it flattered her curves, accentuating it. He felt a strong desire stirring up within him as the bulge between his legs began to get excited. Mentally trying to control his desires, he cleared his throat, "You look, you are...." *"What is wrong with me?"* He muttered to himself. "Are you still hungry?" he managed to say, as he stood up to open one of the dishes. Leya looked at Jay, smiling shyly and walking over to him. She took a look at the array of unopened dishes before her. "See food I only see in magazines" Leya giggled as she opened each dish. Jay moved to sit down, she sat on the couch next to him and put a forkful of food in her mouth. "Good?" He asked. She nodded with the food in her mouth, unable to speak, as they both chuckled.

The night flew by quickly. It was filled with laughter, lots of laughter! Jay wondered who this stranger was that ignited a fire within him. He was overwhelmed by a deep longing for her and a sense of curiosity. Morning had broken and it was time to let her go as arranged, but why did he not want her to leave? He got out of the bathroom to see Leya sleeping beautifully, her hair sprawled all over her face. The t-shirt rumpled up to her crotch revealing her red lace panties as she lay one head on the pillow and her arm clutched another pillow like a little child with its favourite teddy. God! She was gorgeous, he thought. He moved closer to look at her and sat on the bed next to her, stretching his hands to stroke her hair and clearing it protectively from her face. The gesture wakened Leya who looked at him with sleepy eyes and smiled. "Good morning" she said, consciously trying to adjust her hair and shirt. He stared at her quietly for a few seconds and said almost in a whisper, "You're very beautiful." Once again, that awkward moment of silence filled the room. Jay cleared his throat, "Uh, I'm here for one more day. Have lunch with me." "Can't you say please?" she asked eyeing him up in a pretentious frown. He laughed! "Sorry your majesty! Will you do me the honour of having lunch with me please?" He replied chuckling. Leya yawned, nodding in approval. "I'd love to, but, I have to go home and freshen up first." "Of course" Jay responded getting up, the hotel's white towel wrapped around his waist and athletic frame right in her full glare. He stared at her in silence for what felt like eternity and sat on the bed next to her again, stretching his hands towards her hair, lightly brushing at her face. "You are indeed beautiful." "Thank you" she said, lowering her face to avoid him see her blush. He noticed her blush and smiled. Getting up, he said to her, "I've got a meeting until 12, I'll pick you up?" She nodded again! Suddenly, there was a knock and Jay walked over to open the door as one of the hotel staff entered, "Good morning sir" he said, laying Jay's perfectly ironed white shirt on the sofa. "Thank you Ladi" Jay acknowledged. Ladi bowed, smiling as he walked out.

Leya looked at him as he walked towards her wearing the shirt Ladi had put out. "Who are you?" She asked. "No one" he responded. "That's not true, you cannot be no one. I've noticed the way the staff treat you....." "Nope, that's where you're wrong" he cut in, buttoning his shirt. "I would expect that all guests are treated by the hotel staff as they should be. That way, we retain our clients and we build a strong customer base." "We?" Leya asked sitting up, crossed leg on the bed. He chuckled, sat down again on the bed and said to her, "Okay, you inquisitive cat. My family owns this hotel." Leya gasped holding her hand to her mouth. "I have been the acting director since my Dad passed." "I knew it! I knew it!" she exclaimed in excitement with a sense of achievement like a code breaker. "From the way that local fowl you hired as a front guard was behaving, to the people you met walking in and out of here. I knew you had to be manager or something. Check you out! Oga at the top" playfully hitting him with one of the pillows. He giggled getting up, "I have to hurry and oh......" Jay mentioned, suddenly remembering. He opened his wallet and pulled out a bundle of cash, handing it over to her. She collected it in shock, looking at the money in her hand. She had never seen so much money ever! "That's the sixty thousand as agreed, some extra for your journey back home and the balance of your dressed to kill outfit" he teased, reminding her of the conversation in the elevator. Face flushed, she responded chuckling, "It's not funny!" "Then why are you trying so hard not to laugh" he asked, picking up his blazer. Flinging it over his shoulder, he walked to the door, turned back to look at her and said matter of factly, "Just so you know, I dialled my phone with yours. You have my number now" and walked out.

3

"God put us here, on this carnival ride. We close our eyes never knowing where it'll take us next" – Carrie Underwood

66 Issa lie! Leyaaaa" Bunmi shouted excitedly, holding Leya by her shoulders and shaking her just as she finished narrating the turn of the night's event. Bunmi moved to sit on their worn out double size bed, it's two front wooden legs ready to give way at any moment. "We cannot let this one go oh. Hah! See as I am counting money that we did not even whine waist for," she said flipping through the money in her hands. "Bunmi, the guy is fineeeeeee" Leya stressed as she fell on to the bed with dreamy eyes, her face looking up the ceiling. "See this one" Bunmi

gestured at her. "Don't come and fall in love o. These ones are not our level, na to chop the money go. Ehen I cooked beans, Oya co....." Bunmi did not finish her sentence when Leya interjected, "Which beans? I am going out to lunch you say beans." "It is not your fault" Bunmi responded, playfully hitting Leya on the bed with the wad of cash in her hands. Suddenly, they heard heavy bangs on their door and Bunmi turned towards the door as Leya sat up! "Who is that?" Bunmi yelled angrily, "Do you want to break my door?" The banging continued even louder. Angrily, she walked towards the door muttering, "You will be there o, one devil will just come and start looking for your trouble." She opened the door and it was Charity again, the extremely slender, call girl with defined high cheeks and jaw bone with visible tattoos on her chest and arm who lived in the same compound. Charity was what others would refer to as skinny but she loved her body. In her eyes, she was Africa's next top model and you could tell her nothing. The rivalry between Charity and Bunmi was inexplicable. They simply could not stand each other and it was a known fact amongst the other girls. "I said it now!" Bunmi said angrily, looking at Charity, ready to pounce on her. "I said it! That it will be one devil who will just be looking for your wahala." Leya stretched her neck to see who was at the door, she shook her head nonchalantly and put her head back down on the bed. "Bunmi, where is my pant?" Charity asked, hands on her hip, tapping her right foot spoiling for a fight. "Pant keh?" Bunmi started to laugh and clapped her hands simultaneously. "Heyyy, is like your village people are using your head to play ball so sense have finished." Leya let out a muffled laugh on the bed. "Charity, I said is like your village people..." Charity interrupted, "It is your own village people using your head to play ball. Thief!! Ordinary pant you cannot buy, you are now stealing people's pant on the drying line." Bunmi burst into uncontrollable laughter. "So if I want to steal ashawo's pant, I will not find any pant o, it is this walking stick's pant abi?" she asked pointing at Charity's body from head to toe. "See my nyash" Bunmi pointed, turning around to reveal her rather large round perky behind. "See your own nyash wey be like flat plate. How your pant go come fit me?" Bunmi asked. "Don't insult me o, don't insult me. Just bring out my pant. You want to go and use my pant for ritual" Charity shouted, moving closer to Bunmi. "Charity, if I slap you ehnnn, I said if I hammer that your........" Bunmi's attention diverted to the other girls in the compound as

29

one held a black lace panties that looked like it had seen better days. There were visible small holes and the crotch area faded into a greyish colour. "Who get this pent? This one no be pant o, na pent" the girl shouted, raising the underwear with one finger disgustingly as the other girls laughed hysterically. "See as pant don fade!" She continued. Charity's attention moved towards the loud laughter and angrily walked to the girls. "You're lucky" she called out to Bunmi as she walked away. Bunmi laughed, "See this one o! Until I mash your face like porridge. You go hear word and respect." Charity grabbed her pant from the girl aggressively and walked to her room leaving the other girls in fits of laughter.

Leya ignoring the commotion going on in the compound, was getting ready in the room when her phone rang. She looked at the number curiously and picked up. "Hello," she answered. "Heyyy" Jay responded in a sexy drool. "For some strange reason, you've been on my mind all morning. You okay? Paid off your debt yet?" He asked chuckling. Leya giggled, walking towards the window and drawing the curtain to see Bunmi and the girls having a conversation in continuous fits of laughter. "I'm okay and yes, I have paid my debt" She responded. "Looks like someone's having fun." Jay said, hearing the loud laughs over the phone. "Fun? No oh, just a daily occurrence in this compound. Fight fight fight every day." Leya pointed out as Jay chuckled. "So, I'll see you at 1:30?" he asked. "Sure." Leya responded, picking up her hair brush. "The infamous Gbese house right?" Leya laughed. "Yes, the infamous Gbese house" She confirmed. He hung up, looking at his phone for a few seconds. Smiling, he turned on his car ignition.

Bunmi entered the room to see Leya applying her red lipstick. "See fineeeee girl. See Babe! No beauty pass your own" Bunmi teased her lovingly. Leya laughed, "My hype woman B!" Bunmi started to walk lopsided around the room hip pop style, gesturing like a hip hop artist, "You know how we do," they broke down in laughter. Silently, Leya asked "Do you think I'm overly dressed?" looking at her herself in her white lace body suit tucked into her slightly ripped mom jeans and red blazer rolled up to her arms. As she held her hair into a messy high bun with strands hanging on the sides of her face and a bang over her forehead, Bunmi walked over to Leya, holding her by the shoulders and looking at her, "Baby girl, you look perfect!" hugging her.

31

Gbese house *translated as Debt House in the Yoruba language* also popularly known as G House, was right in the middle of the ghetto. It was a highly undesirable, dirty, crime ridden area. A dilapidated building that had been turned into a brothel where men came and went at various times of the day. It was a large compound, all ten rooms facing each other with two toilets and bathrooms which had broken door handles. There was a large hole at the bottom of one of the wooden doors of the bathroom which was a delight for the many rats who shared the compound with the girls. It was normal for the girls to have their baths with a rat perched in a corner of the bathroom. Jay arrived at Gbese house looking around through his windscreen, the pungent smell from the surrounding gutters so strong, it came through the ventilation in his vehicle. Don Dadaa, an average height, rough looking street hoodlum, hair in knots, bare chested with a cigarette stick stuck between his ear noticed Jay as he parked by Gbese house. He walked towards the car, touching it in a sweep motion and walking in lopsided swagger. Talking to himself and jumping in elation, he exclaimed excitedly, "Ooomoh see machine. See carrrr, ah!" Jay pressed a button and the window rolled down. "You good?" He asked. "Hah, boss! I hail o. How far na? You dey look for person?" Don responded, taking his cigarette from his ear." "Yeah actually. I'm here to pick up someone." Don Dadaa looked at him surprised, "You come look for person from Gbese house? Na ashawo full there na?" Jay smiled, "I know." He looked at a distracted Don Dadaa who was searching through his pockets. "Abeg you get lighter?" He asked Jay. "No, I don't smoke." "Boss boss, das why you fresh reash this kain level. For here ehn, man must smoke something if you wan reason. Anyway sha, we fit come into agreement" he said, looking at the car and smiling. "Sorry, what?" Jay asked confused. "I say, organise something s3h! You see ehnn, there is hunger in the land o. As you come out from this machine now, enter G house, by the time you don come back, you see those boys wey dey dia" pointing to a group of hoodlums smoking, laughing and occasionally looking over at Jay and his car. Jay looked over at them, Don Dadaa continued, "As you enter G house, tyre don comot, side mirror don disappear, engine, hah! Engine, go don vanish tey tey. Infact ehnn, dem go dissect this machine, car seat sef no go remain." Jay looked over at them again, one made eye contact with him and winked. Jay turned back to Don. "Your name is....." "Haaah, queeestion!!" he replied, moving around like a rap artiste on stage. "My name na Don Dadaa, the only don for this area. The head boy in charge. After me nobody..." he praised himself. "But just call me Don, I go answer." "Okay Don" Jay mentioned, reaching into his trouser pocket and bringing out a wad of cash handing it over to him, "Protect my machine." Don looked at Jay, and then at the bundle of cash in his hands as Jay turned to walk towards the house. He shouted, "Hah! Poverty, you're a baastarrrd!"

The girls in Gbese house were deeply engaged in conversation and making fun of their customers – a usual routine where they gathered outside their rooms exchanging tales of their escapades and various night walks. One of the girls, Agatha, holding a bottle of beer in one hand and smoking a cigarette stuck between her two fingers continued, "That is how the idiot come lie on top person pikin, one minute no even enter sef, one minute, Oga say baby I'm coming, I'm coming" mimicking her customer, pretending to tremble. The girls burst out laughing. They all turned towards Jay as he walked into the compound and in a split second, ran simultaneously towards him. Some of the girls touched him provocatively, others simply admired him. "See fine boyyyy," one of the girls said to him, running her hands up and down his arm. "I can give you an amazing time" another cut in.

****

"I don't know", Leya said looking deflated. "What am I even doing?" She asked Bunmi. "What you are doing baby girl, is securing the bag" Bunmi responded, giving her a playful pinch. "Ouch" Leya winced, touching her arm when their attention drew to the noise outside. Bunmi walked over to the window looking out and shouted, "Blood of Jesus! Not these brood of vipers!" quickly walking out the door. "Hey! Hey! Hey!" she cautioned, walking towards them, "By the count of three, let me not see any child of misfortune standing here." "Ah ah, what is it now?" Agatha asked as she took a long inhale of her cigarette and puffed into thin air. "What is what? Are you expecting visitor, you fit get visitor wey be like this?" Bunmi asked, looking at Jay and smiling at him admiringly. Jay looked on at them, hands in his pockets. The girls began to disperse, some muttered insults under their breath but dared not say it out loud to incur Bunmi's wrath. Bunmi looked at Jay quietly, assessing him up and down as Jay cleared his throat uncomfortably. "Hi, I'm here to see......"

"Leya" Bunmi interrupted! He looked surprised that she knew. "That's my girl mehnnnn, very correct chick! Not all these things you are seeing" she gestured towards the other girls who had formed into small groups looking at Jay and Bunmi. "Leya will be out....." she had not finished her sentence when she noticed Jay's gaze affixed on something intensely. She followed his gaze to see Leya walking towards them. In that moment, time froze and Jay was transported into a world of emotion. She got to where they stood and the irresistible smell of her cheap perfume, the soft airiness and strong musk immersed him in the sweetness of the moment as he looked at her with such warmth and said a soft "Hi." "Hi," she replied, looking at him almost shy. He always looked at her in a way that made her weak at the knees. Who was this man? Why did he make her feel like every ounce of her breath was being taken from her, floating away in the deep blue sky like beautiful butterflies? Bunmi looked at Jay and then at Leya, she smiled! "You ready?" He asked, stretching his hand to her. "Yes," she replied, taking his hand. As they turned to leave, Leya said abruptly startling Jay, "Wait!" She ran to Bunmi and gave her a nervous tight hug. "You got this" Bunmi whispered, as Leya walked backwards, smiling at Bunmi, before turning to

36

hold Jay's hand. She passed her arm through his as they walked out.

Don Dadaa had stood by Jay's Velar in full guard when a young guy passed by. He looked at it admiringly and tried to touch it when Don Dadaa moved towards him, his hand raised to slap him. "I go wound you if you touch this machine." "Ah ah, e never reach to wound person now. I just dey check am" the guy said apologetically. "Check wetin? My friend comot for here before I sound check your ear." The young man looked at Don in trepidation and walked away shaking his head. Don Dadaa saw Jay and Leya walking towards him and gathered his composure, adjusting his imaginary shirt. "Oga di Oga. No other Oga" he said saluting and bowing to Jay. Jay shook his hand and said thank you. "Ah no wahala sir, I dey for you. Any day you come this area. Bring Farari sef, no body go fit touch am as long as I dey here" he responded with a wide smile. Don Dadaa's attention turned to Leya. "Leya mama" he said smiling and moving around her in sheer admiration. "I talk am! I talk am say if this Oga enter G house, the only person wey fit level am small na Leya because ehnnn, all those other girls....." Don continued, making a face. Jay chuckled and cut in, "Anyways, we've got to go now" he said, walking to open the door for Leya. "No problem baba. Make me sef go Mama Risika place, condemn some hot amala and cold beer with enough shaki, cowleg, roundabout, dry fish. Hah! Enjoyment" Don exclaimed, flipping the cash Jay gave him and giving them some dance moves. Jay laughed as he got into his car, "Nice meeting you Don" he said, as Don saluted. "At your service any time sir" he responded. He watched as Jay and Leya drove off, quickly hiding the money in his boxers and looking around to make sure no one was watching. He walked away wiping his mouth with his face towel smiling.

"Food, glorious food" - Anonymous

They arrived at one of the city's upscale restaurant that served only the elite in society. Leya felt a bit awkward as she looked around. The atmosphere, lighting, art work and spacing created some sort of intimacy which was almost romantic. She was used to the local restaurants and road side food sellers, this setting and its decor was an unusual experience for her. As the waiter led them to their seats presenting them with the menu, Jay kept looking at her. Why was he filled with nervous anticipation? He was so excited, even a bit giddy like a school boy meeting his crush. Leya caught him staring, "You have such an intense stare" she said embarrassed. "Does that make you uncomfortable?" He asked. "Yes, no, I mean...." she answered nervously and he laughed. The waiter walked over to them with a bottle of wine, Jay took the bottle from him and poured Leya a glass. Taking a sip, she asked nonchalantly, "So who was that girl?" "Which girl?" Jay asked slightly confused. "The one you met by the elevator." "Oh, Ify" Jay confirmed. "Just someone I know." "Hah! It's a lie jor. The way sis was playing with her hair? Abeg abeg!" Jay laughed, refilling her glass. "Okay, someone I dated a while ago." "Do you want to get me drunk?" Leya asked looking at her refilled glass. Jay smiled, "A woman's glass should never be empty" he responded. They stared at each other, quietly, when the waiter returned and served their lunch. Leya looked at the palatable beetroot braised rice with the spicy lamb chops before her and took a forkful of her food. "Ummmmm" she exclaimed in delight, closing her eyes. Jay chuckled, "Delicious?" He asked. She nodded, eyes still closed. Moments later, she opened her eyes to see Jay having just a warm beef salad. "Will this fill you up?" She asked curiously. Jay looked down at his food and then looked up at her, "Yup" he replied. "You these rich people sef!" Leya said rolling her eyes as she put another forkful of food in her mouth, savouring the taste. Jay watched her eat, his mind racing. He liked this girl! He wanted more of her. "Ehen, Ify" Leya started, remembering her earlier question. The delicious food and its aroma had transported her senses to another world that she had momentarily forgotten everything else but the food. Jay moved his head back in laughter, "You curious cat! Okay, yes, we did see each other a few times, her family are in the interior decor business and yes....." Jay continued when Leya cut in. "So, why did you ask me out to lunch? Are you even....." "Because you intrigue me Leya" Jay interrupted, staring at her. "There's something about you that makes me want to know more...."

Leya looked away from him and nervously played with her food. She liked him too, *he seemed different*, she thought to herself. Taking a sip of his drink and putting it down, he said to her, "It's my last night at the hotel. Would you like to spend the night with me?" Leya looked up at him and asked, "All night? It will......." "Cost me, I know" Jay finished, smiling at her.

The afternoon had flown by, too quickly in fact! They had enjoyed each other's company, laughing, talking about everything and anything. He felt at peace with her! The call girl he had met unexpectedly the night before. The drive back to The Point hotel was in total silence that one could hear a pin drop! Occasionally, they stole glances at each other and smiled. As they arrived at the hotel, Bayo the front guard spotted his boss and a lady. Recognising Leya from the previous night, he opened his mouth so wide it could catch a fly and shouted in shock. "Ah, Oga Daniels! Oga! Ashawo? God forbid!" he said to himself, shrugging his shoulders. Inside the hotel, Jay slotted in his card and the door to his suite opened, automatically turning on the lights. He gestured towards a seat and asked Leya, "Drink?" She nodded sitting down. *"Back here again"* she thought to herself, looking around admiring the suite just as she did the first time she saw this beauty. "So, question for you. Why do you not kiss or give you know...." Jay said walking towards Leya and handing her the drink. She took a sip, Jay sat next to her. "Welllll" she stressed, "I think kissing comes with strong emotions, you can't just go round kissing everyone. There must be some emotional connection to want to kiss someone and my job involves no emotional connection at all. You pay me, I lie down, you do your thing and I fake an orgasm. Job done!" "You've never had a real orgasm?" Jay asked surprised. "No" Leya responded truthfully.

41

"Wow" he muttered. "No time for all that! I finish one customer, on to the next, bills to pay. I get home tired, sleep, start all over" she responded matter of factly. "And your stance on your, you know, not to be touched and giving......" Jay asked as Leya cut in, "...head?" She laughed out loud. "Hah! I cannot be going round sucking every man now. Ah ah! No. And your business is not with my vagina, all you need is the hole abi? Ehen! If I would ever engage in oral sex, then there must be that......" "Emotional connection!" Jay completed her sentence. She looked away blushing! Blushing? Goodness! Why was this man making her blush? Men meant nothing to her – she made sure of that! So, why was this man trying to take her Queendom? Who was he? How dare he? This was a job, and a job it should be! "Can we start?" She blurted out, standing and beginning to undress. Jay looked at her, taken aback by her action as she took her blazer off. His gaze intensified as she unbuttoned her trouser, taking them off. She stood before him, her skin so glossy, her body contoured in all the right places. God! She was utterly beautiful, Jay thought. Leya's white lace body suit did not do much to cover her perk round breasts, her areola visible through the miniature nets of the lace. She loosened her hair and it fell all over her

42

shoulder in the sexiest way. Jay felt a powerful stir through him, a strong desire burning within. He got up, walked over to her and ran his fingers through her hair, staring at her body slowly, and every gaze piercing through her. He arched his head as if to give her a kiss but moved on to slowly brush at her chin and then her ears. She closed her eyes and inhaled gently, her heart beating. She wasn't meant to feel this way, this was a job. Her job did not involve the soft touches and caresses so why was she enjoying his hands move down to her breast, slightly cupping them and then to her hips, slowly caressing her body. He nibbled and kissed her neck gently, his lips moving back to her chin as she slightly arched her neck to the side ready for the next sensual stirring this man was doing to her. Suddenly he stopped!

She opened her eyes almost disappointed! He looked into them and said quietly, "I don't have sex, I make love. To make love to you, I have to kiss you. Make you want me as much as I want you." He looked at her from her chest downwards, "I'm attracted to you. God! I don't know what it is" he said putting one hand on his head as he tried to speak, pacing up and down. "....there's something about you. Something! And I want more." he said, looking at her as she stood as still as a statue watching him. Jay

43

walked towards her, taking one of her hands into his, covering it with his other hand. "Move in with me" He proposed, his look stern. She looked at him stunned. "I know! I just met you and it sounds ridiculous but I'd love the company, and to be honest, I don't like you living with those girls." Finally able to speak, Leya said quietly, "but Bunmi is....." "Bunmi is nice and seems like she has your best interest at heart" he interrupted her. She let go of her hand, looking at him suspiciously and exclaimed, "What if you're a ritualist?" "Ritual what?" He laughed. Chuckling, he took her hand again, "No, I'm not a ritualist. I'm not after your blood or anything sinister. I just want to get to know you." She let go of her hand again and went to take a seat, "How can you want to know a prostitute" she asked. "I'm a call girl, ashawo. I sleep with men for money. You seem to not get it. You're extremely hot and obviously rich. You can get any woman you want." She continued. "And that's exactly what I'm doing" he responded, looking at her.

"Prepare your mind to receive the best that life has to offer"
– Ernest Holmes

Leya told Bunmi about Jay's offer as they folded clothes from the communal drying line. "You remember what I told you the first day I met you?" Bunmi asked. Leya smiled, "When sister Charity of life was fighting me for that foolish taxi driver customer who eventually chopped her and cleaned mouth." They both laughed at the memory. "I told you, you didn't belong here." Bunmi stopped folding the blouse she had in her hands and playfully hit Leya with it. "He is not a stranger now. We know his name, we know what family he belongs to, we know what businesses he owns. He cannot try any nonsense. I will just arrange Don Dadaa and his boys to go and sort him out jare." She said, as she proceeded to fold the blouse. "Besides, you know I'm always here. I no dey go anywhere. Abeggie go chop make me sef chop." "Bunmiiiii" Leya exclaimed, looking at her in a pretentious frown. "What? The guy likes you." Bunmi responded. "You know we are not in the same class Bunmi" Leya warned. "And so?" Bunmi hissed, rolling her eyes.

Later in the day, Bunmi had helped Leya pack all her life belongings into the one medium suitcase she owned. Dressed in a white anglais broderie mini lace smock dress, her hair in two cute plaits laying down on each side of her shoulder and her red matte lipstick, Bunmi looked at her admiringly. "I said it, you don't belong here. Just look at you." Leya smiled nervously. "Don't worry, everything will be just fine" Bunmi assured her as they heard a knock on their door. They both turned to look as Bunmi went to open the door. "Hi" she said, smiling at Jay, admiring him from head to toe. *"This guy fine o"* she thought. "Hey Bunmi" Jay replied. "Is Leya...." he had not finished asking when Leya walked up to them. He smiled at her with such warmth, she blushed. "You look beautiful! As always" he said almost in a whisper, admiring Leya's look. "Thanks" Leya responded, embarrassed like a teenager meeting her idol. "You ready?" he asked, she nodded. Jay took Leya's suitcase as she hugged and kissed Bunmi on the cheek. He placed his hand around her waist as they left the house she had always known, an emotional Bunmi watching and waving. The G house girls looked on, some clearly jealous and others in admiration.

4

" Take the first step in faith. You don't have to see the whole staircase, just take the first step" – Martin Luther King Jnr

Leya could not believe she had just woken up in Jay's home. It was a large gated detached house with a section that housed his exotic cars. The lawn was perfectly mowed with a garden swing positioned on the left side of the driveway. His bedroom had a large chesterfield king size bed with a headboard that matched his sheets, 2 black and chrome bedside lamps standing beautifully on silver mirrored drawers on each side of the bed. He had an ensuite as large as the room she shared with Bunmi and a walk in wardrobe the size of the hotel room they first met at. The floor of the house was marbled and the home's interior decor was very contemporary with a touch of elegance that brought timeless sophistication to it. Each piece of accessory complemented the furniture and colour theme. Leya had taken up on his offer – after all, she had nothing to lose and even more to gain, like a nice warm bed and luxurious comfort she only saw in movies. She was not exactly sure where this was going for they were two totally different individuals in every sense of the word.

The perfect ray of morning sunlight shone through the venetian blinds in the bedroom. Jay was in the large walk in wardrobe, trying on a shirt ready for work when Leya entered, slightly running her hand around his waist. She sat on the drawer work top in front of him obstructing his view of the mirror and began to button his shirt without saying a word. "Had a good night?" He asked looking at Leya wearing his bathrobe, her hair dishevelled all over her face in the most enticing way. She nodded, smiling like a little girl. Who wouldn't? For the first time in her life, she had experienced the joy of a comfortable bed in all its splendour. "Good," he replied, stretching his neck to look at the buttoned shirt in the mirror. Leya stared at him adorably. "What?" He asked smiling. "You're forming gentleman for me abi? Why didn't you let us do?" She asked coyly as Jay let out a short laugh, "I told you, I cannot make love to you if I cannot kiss you! And by God, I want to kiss you breathless" he said looking at her, those deep looks he gave her that made something funny go through her tummy – butterflies they called it. Feeling her tummy flutter, the atmosphere turned tense as they both stared at each other in silence, a fleeting moment that felt like a lifetime. "So, what do I do in this big house when you go out to work?" She asked, awkwardly breaking the silence. He replied nonchalantly, pulling the drawers to select a watch, "Go shopping." "Shopping? I can't shop all day now. That's boring." He turned to look at her, "You're the first woman who finds shopping all day boring" he said buckling his Tag Heuer V4 limited edition watch. Still sitting on the work top, she put her hand on her exposed thighs, watching him get ready, the oversized bathrobe falling off her shoulder. "I might just call Bunmi up and have lunch with her." "Good idea" he responded facing her and placing both hands on her bare thighs. She looked around the walk in wardrobe, "How do you know you won't come back to find anything in this your fine house?" Leya mentioned, a mischievous look on her face. "Are you trying to rob me?" He asked chuckling. "You're laughing! It doesn't bother you that you're harbouring a complete stranger?" She asked amazed. "Nope" he replied unbothered. "What kind of a man are you?" Leya asked wondering. "The kind that believes if you've never lost your mind, then you've never followed your heart" he responded. "So, here I am, and the G house girl with the back tattoo" Jay teased. Leya chuckled, "I bought puff puff one day and the paper wrap had a picture of one oyibo chic with a tattoo. To form hard girl now, I decided to get one. That day, Bunmi had to follow me to make sure the area guy, one local champion like that, was not drawing nonsense at my back. For me, the black stars represent my darkest days and the plain stars represent strength and courage. That someday, I'll find hope" Leya smiled painfully. "So, what about finding love?" he asked, his voice husky. Leya was silent! She did not know how to answer that. Suddenly, he stretched his hand to touch her bare shoulder. Leya began to fill the tightening sensation in her tummy again, those flutters. Tracing her collar bone with his fingers, he moved his hand down to her chest, slightly touching her breast. As he arched his head forward to kiss her, he stopped. Recalling their conversation, he apologised and kissed her forehead. "Speak later?" he asked. She shook her head forcing a smile, watching him as he left. She wanted him to kiss her!

****

"Ah, na wa o. So this man meets you, takes a liking to you, asks you to move into his house, gives you money a few times and he has still not forced himself on you?" Bunmi asked Leya as they went through the clothes on the racks at a nearby boutique. She had asked Bunmi to come hang out with her and trust Bunmi never to miss a good time, she had agreed without hesitation. Leya could not believe what was happening and what the next day will bring but she liked this change. Leya shrugged at Bunmi's question. "You sure say this man no get problem? His banana no fit stand ni?" Bunmi asked astonished. Leya giggled, "Trust me, his banana stands very well" as she picked an outfit admiring it before placing it to her body. "So what is it then?" Bunmi asked. "When you meet him ehnnn, please ask him" Leya replied to Bunmi with side eyes. "Oya, have you gotten all you need?" She asked Bunmi whose hands were already filled with stacks of clothes. Bunmi laughed, "See this girl o. Have you gotten all you need?" she mimicked Leya's voice. Leya chuckled as they walked to the countert, "I was only asking now." The sales associate scanned all the items and mentioned the price. Leya nodded, opening her cross body bag and taking out a card. "Hah! Egbami *meaning help me in the Yoruba language* Baba God! You must answer my own call too. The man even gave her his card! Leyaaaa" Bunmi shouted, playfully pushing her. Leya laughed!

That evening after shopping with Bunmi, Leya decided to do something nice for Jay. Who else would give a stranger a roof over their head without asking for anything in return? In the twinkle of an eye, her life was slowly changing, she felt good within herself. Some kind of peace she had never felt before engulfed her and she liked it. Stirring the sauce in her cooking pan and dabbing a bit on to her palm to taste, she nodded smiling. After all, if she couldn't give him anything, she could cook for him. Bunmi always said she was an amazing cook so why not? She anticipated Jay's return like an excited kid who couldn't wait to show off their new toy. A few minutes later, Jay walked through the door and sniffed curiously.

Leya rushed out of the kitchen bouncing up and down wearing a white t-shirt and bum shorts, holding a ladle. "Welcome home you" she said, standing on her toes and kissing him on the cheek which surprised him in a good way. "Something smells amazing?" he said to her. "I cooked" she answered smiling like a little girl. "Hmmm, you cooked ahhh? What did you cook? By the way, where is my chef?" he asked, looking towards the kitchen and then at her. "Well", she replied, unbuttoning his shirt, "I gave him some time off so I could make something special for you. So, why don't you go upstairs, get changed, come back and see for yourself." She looked at him, *God! He was so hot!* Leya thought. "Sounds like a plan!" Jay smiled as he began to walk towards the stairs. "Oh, by the way, nice shorts" he called out, without looking back at her. She looked down at her shorts, smiled and bounced back into the kitchen.

Jay came downstairs to see the meal all laid out on the dining table. He pulled out a chair to sit and tucked into his food. "Won't you pray?" Leya asked as she pulled out a seat next to him. "Oh!" Jay responded. "You don't know whether I've put jazz *black magic** in the food sef, you want to eat" She teased. "Have you?" Jay replied looking at her as he put a forkful in his mouth. "Ummm, this is gooooood" he stressed, eyes closed, savouring every bite. "You like?" She asked smiling, watching him eat, elbow propped on the table and hand cupping her jaw. He looked at her gently, "I love!" and went back to eating. "You're going on like a woman has never cooked for you before" she said. "Well, the only woman who has cooked for me is my mum. Then again, we had, well, we have a few helps who cook anyways." "What about your girlfriend or wife?" She asked. Laughing, Jay responded, "Wife! I wouldn't ask you to come stay with me if I had a wife would I?" he asked. "Forget that thing" she eyed him. "Is this not Lagos we live in? You're rich now. You can house me here, house wife somewhere else, house side chic in another area and we will all be living in this same Lagos. Abeggie." At this point, Jay almost spat out his drink from laughing. He put his drink down, "Seriously though, you think I'd come home every night to you if I had a wife?" "Okay what about girlfriend" She asked. "We broke up" he answered. "Is she also from a rich home?" She asked. "Yep" he replied, sipping on his drink again. "But why do you rich people always want to marry other rich people. So that we poor people will just be poor'ing dey go. No mix up, just constant hunger in our community." He chuckled, "It's not intentional. It really isn't. It's the places we go, the schools we attend, our hangouts. Surely you meet others who kind'a share the same vibe. You get talking, you like each other. Eventually you find out they are from this home or that and it just goes on like that. I mean think about it, what business would I have going to Ajegunle? I know no one there?" "Now you know me" she answered quietly. They stared at each other deeply in silence – something that had become a regular thing. Leya cleared her throat trying to cut through the tense atmosphere. "I got you something" she said, reaching underneath the table to bring out a gift. "You did?" Jay responded surprised and excited at the same time. "Wasn't expecting anything. I'm usually the giver." "Well, it's your card, so I decided to get you something too" Leya said shrugging her shoulders as Jay chuckled. "Still, I give my card to other ladies and none have ever, ever gotten me a gift" taking the box from Leya and unwrapping it. Exclaiming in excitement at the customised real leather bracelet fastened with gold magnets, he said to her, "Love it." "You do?" She enquired. "Yes! Yessssss" Jay smiled, standing and picking her up in his arms. "Thank you," he whispered, gazing into her beautiful brown eyes. "Thank you too" she muttered, a shyness overcoming her. "For saving me from being with other men for a few coins. You have no idea how happy that makes me feel, thank you." Still in his arms, their bodies began to feel each other's warmth, his arousal rearing its head, a strong bulge pressing hard against her. She moved away from him quickly back to the table, "I'll clear the table and do the dishes. Have a rest." "No!" he replied, taking her hands away from the plate. "You made dinner, I'll sort the dishes in the washer." She looked at him in shock and shouted, "African man? Issa lie." "Well, not your average African man" Jay responded as he picked up the plate to the kitchen leaving her staring at him in awe.

"Let life surprise you" - Anonymous

5

"Passion' a word which involves so many feelings. I feel it when we touch; I feel it when we kiss; I feel it when I look at you. For you are my passion; my one true love." - S. Richardson

Leya was still in bed when Jay brought up a cup of freshly brewed tea to her. They had watched a movie together the night before all cuddled up and she had loved every moment of that level of intimacy. This went beyond the physical, she felt like she could connect with him deeply, and each time he looked at her, she could feel his gaze deep into her soul. Every time he laughed at her joke, she felt alive. "Thank you! Good morning" she said, taking a sip. "Morning" he smiled. Looking at her, he continued, "You're so pretty I forgot what I was going to say" Leya blushed. "Got to run to the office, I have a meeti....." Leya interrupted him. "Do you ever take some time off?" she asked. He let out a short laugh, "Business won't take care of itself you know." "It can" she responded. "You have enough employees working for you." "Well, I still have to be available to ensure things are done right." "I knoww" she replied, reaching out to adjust his collar. "....but I want to spend some time with you" Leya pleaded, looking at him puppy faced. I am tired of calling Bunmi up. "She your only friend? No siblings?" Jay asked surprised. "No" she replied, "Bunmi is all I have." He looked at her and saw a sudden sadness overwhelm her, a look he had never seen before. He was used to the larger than life humorous Leya, but who was this person with pain in her eyes? He lifted up her chin, "Heyyy, are you okay?" She nodded at him and then opened her mouth to say "Yes." "Tell you what? Business can take care of itself today" he said, putting his blazer down. Leya's face lit up.

They spent the day exploring the beautiful sights of Lagos in Jay's convertible, the wind blowing through their hair and grey clouds over their heads. They visited places like the Lekki conservation centre rich in landscape, greenery, and wildlife. Passing through the African shrine and enjoying infectious music and a colourful, vibrant atmosphere. Taking some time out to explore the park, Leya walked barefoot on the grass, her sandals in one hand. Jay tried to do the same but struggled, he had never walked bare footed on dried rough grass before - this was an all-new experience for him. As he struggled to walk, Leya looked at him chuckling, "You this Ajebutter children sef, ordinary grass you cannot walk on," she laughed as Jay gave her a frown. "I'd rather be walking on the beach than going through this pure torture" he winced as each foot touched the sharp edges of the prickly grass. Leya laughed, walked over to him, wrapping her arms tightly around his waist and said, "Okay rich boy! Let's go to the beach then." He smiled and planted a kiss on her forehead without saying a word as he bent to put his loafers back on.

They had walked along the beach holding each other's hands as the waves washed ashore over their bare feet. In silence, they walked, taking in their surroundings that captured the beauty and grandeur of Nigerian culture and art whilst enjoying their view of the Atlantic. I could do this forever, Jay thought to himself as he swung Leya's arms gently. After a few minutes of walking in silence, they settled in the sands. Leya sat cross legged in front of him – her favourite sitting position, with his chest pressed against her back and his arms wrapped around her. He bent to kiss her neck, his lips buried in the crevice of her neck. She closed her eyes and arched her neck to the side as Jay continued to bury his face in her neck, inhaling her perfume. Leya had upgraded her perfume and he had gotten used to the soft lingering feminine scent that was not only delightful, but fresh, exotic and delicious. "You smell so good" he muttered, face still buried in her neck, occasionally nibbling. "Thanks to your debit card" she responded. He laughed! She loved it when he laughed, it was the sexiest thing ever. It was not overpowering or obnoxious, it was a soft velvety laugh, and so smooth it aroused her. She could feel her juices flowing down, her underwear soaking up. For the first time in her life, she wanted a man, this man! "You do something to me" he whispered. The bulge between his legs, hard and pushing against her spine, Leya turned to face him as she stroked his face, her finger tracing the scar. Their gaze were fixed on each other with the only noise coming from the sound of the sea waves. He was different! She had been with him for a while now and had been a complete gentleman. Normally, she was always in control of her emotions, her body and her thoughts, but she was losing all three faster than lightning. Did men like this truly exist or this was all a dream? Her thoughts were interrupted with a loud "Una go buy suya?" A young man in a dirty white, full length kaftan holding a large tray filled with grilled meats sprinkled with a special blend of spices stood over them. He let out a wide grin as they looked at him. "No!" Leya retorted. "Oga, you go buy suya?" The young man asked again, looking at Jay. "Ah, ah! Na force? I said no" Leya responded sharply. "Aunty, no be you I dey ask. Oga...." Leya interrupted again, "Your ear don block abi?" "Aunty, I say no be you I dey ask. You don answer your own already." The Suya seller replied rudely, Jay chuckled. "No, no suya, thanks" he responded to the young man. "Ahaa, see correct man wey im mama born well. See as he answer" the suya seller said, eyeing Leya up. "My friend, if you don't carry this your dirty self from here ehnnn" Leya replied, standing up, ready for a fight. Jay got up swiftly to prevent any escalations as he stood between the suya seller and Leya. "Fine girl, no sense" the suya seller chastised, turning to walk away. Leya moved towards him aggressively but Jay pulled her back. "You're so feisty" he said laughing. "Caalmmm down" he teased, shaking

61

her shoulder. "Leave me jor. You cannot always be forming posh boy o. This country will just drown you" Leya warned. "But I'm not a posh boy" he responded smiling at her. "Story! Have you eaten at a Buka before? Do you even know Buka?" She asked. He laughed, sitting back down on the ground, saying nothing. "See?" She confirmed, sitting facing him, cross legged. Suddenly, his phone rang, he looked at it for a second and answered the call. Leya reached out to take the phone from him, "Mr Daniel's phone, he's not available right now but please leave a message" and cut the call, placing the phone back in his trouser pocket. He looked at her surprised and speechless! Looking at him without saying a word but only a sly smile on her face, she wrapped her arms and legs around him. "You just cut my call," he said. She shrugged her shoulders and kissed him on the cheek, burying her face in his shoulder. *Why was he not mad at her? Why did he think that was the sexiest thing ever?* He thought as he smiled and wrapped his arms around her, eyes closed, listening to the waves of the sea.

****

A day off with Leya turned out to be two days off work. Jay enjoyed her company, her sassiness and wit. She was as real as it got! No pretence about her, which was a far cry from the ladies he knew and dated. He often wondered how a girl like her turned out working the streets. She had come into his life in the strangest and most unexpected way, the prostitute from Gbese house! He loved the sweet little moments they shared like when she lay her head on his shoulder fast asleep, her arms through his, each time they watched a movie. She had taken him to a Buka teaching him to eat the ways of the locals. He struggled a bit but her laughs and the moment she affectionately wiped the dripping sauce from the side of his mouth filled him with a warmth, an intense longing for her. Heart-warming thoughts filled him when he remembered the nights he worked from home on his laptop and Leya would walk in, turning on the volume of the music playing softly in the background and dancing, pretending to be the singer. She was so easy going and he loved that about her! Taking evening drives together, they bopped their heads in the same direction, left, right, left, right as they listened to the music playing on the stereo and burst out laughing at their silliness. They had taken a long drive to the Yankari National Park, visiting the Marshall caves, Wikki warm springs and the over fifty species of rich wildlife. A visit to the Lagos art gallery was a few hours totally lost on Leya. "So, someone will wake up one day and draw this kind of nonsense and hang for people to see and buy?" Leya had asked as she tilted her head sideways trying to understand the painting on the wall. Jay burst out laughing, watching her seriously try to figure out the drawings. "It's abstract art" Jay had explained. "You these rich people sef" Leya said in defeat, giving up and walking away as Jay chuckled, returning to admire the painting on the wall.

****

It was night time with the heavy April rains pouring down, splattering against the windows. Jay was propped up on the bed, bare chested, he had fallen asleep. Leya came out from the bathroom after her evening shower, dressed in a black deep V neck lacy lingerie that accentuated her hips, revealing her cleavage. She moved to sit by Jay, watching him sleep. His heart beating gently, in and out with every breathe he took. Leya carefully took the papers in his hands, placing them on the night stand and then moved closer to his face. She looked at him for a few seconds and then placed her lips on his gently. Stopping to look at him, she placed her lips on his again. She began to experiment with his lips, learning to kiss him. The movement on Jay's lips awakened him as he looked at Leya startled, she stopped! He stared at her quietly, his look intense as he reached out to touch his lips with hers, kissing her passionately. He had waited for this moment, this time where he could taste her lips, tickle her tongue with his. Jay stopped kissing her for a brief second, looked into her eyes and began to pull the lingerie strap off her shoulder. His hands slid down her chest, cupping her right breast, grazing his thumb over her nipple. Still kissing her, he began to undress her.

Jay positioned her properly on the bed, a deep passion filled his eyes as he watched her beautiful naked body right before him. The touch of his hands on her bare skin sent shivers through her body. He traced her nipple with his tongue in circular motions before placing it in his mouth as he sucked on it as delicately as a flower, gently squeezing her breast. What was he doing to her? How did these parts of her body bring pleasure she knew nothing about? He moved up to kiss her again and trail his tongue down her neck to her belly button and lingered down to her woman.

She let out a deep moan as he took her into his mouth, sucking, licking and tongue thrusting into her. Leya was losing her mind! Her moans were as loud as the thunder that came with the falling rain. Jay was filled with unreserved passion and fire surged through him each time she moaned. He loved to hear her moan, her pleasure was paramount, and he made sure of that! Leya could feel her body trembling like electric bolts running through her blood and veins. Jay lifted his head up to look at her as he passed his fingers through hers, squeezing them as he thrust into her slowly, she gasped! Feeling the fullness of him inside her as he thrust in and out, she wrapped her legs around him. A deep hunger grew within him, feeling her woman with each thrust, warm and wet. He thrust harder, groaning, as the thunder rumbled. This was the moment, just the two of them, making love to one another. Leya spread her hands across the muscles on his chest, stroking it. She lifted her body from the bed with him still inside of her and pushed his back against the headboard as she sat facing him, striding and gyrating her hips in the continuous passionate throes of love making. With their arms wrapped around each other, her lips caressing his neck, nibbling at his ear lobe and the crevice behind his ear. Jay could feel his body shudder, his tense muscles momentarily going weak. He held Leya tight as his fingers curved into her back in the moment of their climax, falling on the bed as Leya's body continued to tremble.

Minutes later, Leya lay on a very sleepy Jay's chest, his arm around her, their naked bodies pressed against each other. "So this is what an orgasm feels like" she said, kissing his chest. "Huh?" He responded half asleep. "Let's do it again" she said striding him. They made love into the early hours of the morning, ending up on the floor with Jay fast asleep. Leya climbed atop him, kissing all over his face. Her soft kisses stirred his senses, waking him up. "Leyaaaa, you're trying to kill me" he said smiling, his eyes closed. "Well, Mr Daniels, it's all your fault" she said to him. He responded to her kisses eyes still closed. In between her kisses, he muttered, "Someone give me food, pleaseeee." Leya laughed, her elbow propped on his chest. "What do you want to eat?" "I could eat a cow right now" he replied. "A whole cow?" She asked laughing and he nodded. "Alright then" she said, picking up the blanket next to her to cover her naked body. He pulled her back down as she got up, kissing her. It was slow, deep and meaningful, "You can go now" he whispered seductively. Leya got up smiling, he closed his eyes and turned to his side to sleep.

"It is a risk to love. What if it doesn't work out? Ah, but what if it does" – Peter McWilliams

6

"Someday, someone will walk into your life and make you realise why it never worked out with anyone else" – Shon Mehta

Leya had so many beautiful reasons to be happy! She had accepted where she was in life and was making the most out of each day. It felt good not to have walked the streets for months and to top it all, the dashing gentleman whose beautiful home she shared, kept giving her the most mind blowing orgasm! The first man she ever kissed on the lips.

She was in the kitchen – her favourite place in the house, when she heard a knock on the door. Wondering who it was, she went to check as whoever it could be, kept knocking and ringing the bell incessantly. Leya opened the door and standing before her was a fair skinned lady, clutching a black Chanel quilted lambskin handbag and dressed in an asymmetric midi dress in burnt sienna that fell off her shoulder, with a thigh high slit revealing more skin. Her middle part lace wig fell over her bare shoulder in large luscious curls. She had an air about her that did not resonate well with Leya. "Hello" Leya said. "Who are you?" the lady responded, brushing past Leya and waltzing into the house, her heels clicking. "Jay, Jayyyy," she called out, looking around and walking up to the edge of the stairs, looking up. "He's not here" Leya answered. She turned to give Leya a haughty look and asked, "Then where is he?" "Who are you?" Leya asked. She sized Leya up and let out a short rude laugh. "Who am I?" she mocked. "My name is Amara and I am Jay's girlfriend." *Ahhh, so this was the Amara Jay told her about? What a stuck up bitch she was,* Leya thought to herself. "Now who are you?" Amara asked, her nose up in the air. Leya looked at her matter of factly and walked away to the kitchen ignoring her. "Excuse me? How dare you walk away when I'm still talking to you? Hey, hey" Amara called out to Leya. She sat down crossing her leg, wondering who Leya was. "How dare she walk away from me" Amara muttered to

70

herself. Minutes after she arrived, the sound of a car parking in the driveway could be heard. "Guess babe's home" Amara said smiling. "I'll be making sure that rude thing leaves today" she continued to speak herself, looking towards the kitchen. Jay walked in spotting Amara who rushed over to hug him. He stopped her with his arm stretched out, "What're you doing here?" He asked in a firm tone. "Oh, hi Amara, so happy to see you too" Amara responded sarcastically at Jay. "I said, what're you doing here?" He repeated angrily. "Here to see my man of course, that's what I'm doing." "I'm not your man" Jay said looking at Amara. He turned his head to see Leya propped against the kitchen door watching. He walked over to her, staring at her warmly for a few seconds, before kissing her sweetly on the lips. "You okay?" He asked, almost in a whisper. Leya nodded in a half smile. "Good!" he responded smiling, and walked back to Amara staring at him in shock. "Really Jay? In my fucking presence?" She yelled angrily. "Now" he said, picking up her bag and grabbing her by the arm, "You're leaving." "I'm going nowhere Jason Daniels, nowhere" loosening herself from his grip. "You think this is some sort of game to you Amara?" he asked. "You show up one day, say we should break up, you want to travel the world and feel suffocated in this relationship. Come back after a few months, begging you made a mistake. Then you try to get your friend to make a pass at me, basically set me up to test our relationship. You are constantly trying to sabotage whatever it is we had! What the hell do you want from me?" He yelled at her. "You Jay, you" she yelled back! "I want you" she exclaimed more calmly. "Yes admitted, I have been foolish a few times but....." she said reaching to touch him. "I don't care whether you have been foolish or not. You play too many games and its tiring" he replied. "Is this about her?" Amara pointed to Leya still calmly watching the spectacle from the kitchen entrance. "Leave her out of this" Jay warned. Amara laughed! "I see you have downgraded! Beautiful no doubt but you can smell a bloody commoner from a distance" snorted Amara, looking at Leya in disgust! "That's it!" Jay exclaimed, grabbing Amara and her bag. "Get out and stay out!" He shouted, pushing her out the door and flinging her bag at her. He shut the door, locking it. "I'll be back Jay, this is not the end. Aunty E will hear about this" Amara yelled, banging on the door. Leya had watched the whole drama and her heart was fuzzy for this man! She could not believe he, who was clearly out of her league had stood up for her. Leya had never had anyone stand up for her except Bunmi and this made her heart melt. He walked over to her and quietly took her in his arms, kissing her forehead and wrapping his arms around her. She felt safe!

"Keep your heels, head and standards high" – Coco Chanel

Elena Daniels was a classy, sophisticated middle aged woman always adorned in beautiful jewellery and clothes. She had the allure of a woman in full possession of herself, a force to be reckoned with. No doubt, Elena was the matriarch of the Daniels family and very committed to ensuring their legacy continued. She was always impeccably dressed with the finest jewels on her neck or wrist in bare minimum, believing less was more. Studying in one of the most renowned universities in England, she had met Jay's father and there, a relationship had formed leading to many years of marriage and a business conglomerate together. Jay was at their exceptionally beautiful family home, at the invitation of his mum for lunch. "Mum, mummmm" he called out, as he stepped into the living room. "Hey baby" she responded, walking over to hug him. His face lit up as he gave her a kiss on the cheek. "Sorry honey, I was tending to the flowers in the garden. Bassey does a terrible job with them" she said, sitting down. "Not sure why you still hire him" Jay giggled. "What can I do my darling, I owe it to your dad. Promised him I was going to keep Bassey until he retired. Now, the man is retired but he still would not leave." Jay laughed! She looked at him in admiration, her son, she was so proud of him! After being told by the doctors, following a very complicated pregnancy, that she could not have any more children, she had raised him with heart, soul and fire. Seeing him sit across her, she knew she had done a good job, despite attempts by his dad to spoil him silly to her dismay. "So, how have you been?" she asked, crossing her legs and looking at him with so much affection. "Never been great" he replied, relaxing into the chair in an almost content state. "I seeeee" his mum said, looking at him with a suspicious smile. "What?" He asked smiling. "Nothing," she responded, reaching out to pick up a magazine. "Mum, stop it" "Stop what?" she feigned ignorance. "You know what I'm talking about. I know Amara has been here with her emotional blackmail, which is why you invited me to lunch" he said looking at her coyly. "Ah Amara!" his mum sighed. "Poor girl came here crying her eyes out." Jay rolled his eyes shaking his head. "She met another lady at yours I understand." "Damn right she did!" "Language, young man!" His mum sternly interrupted, he apologised. "Amara needs to grow up and yes she met someone else." "And who is this someone else?" His mum enquired. "Well, just someone who gives me peace," he smiled. "Interesting" his mum echoed, gesturing to one of the staff to pour her a drink. The staff attempted to pour Jay a drink but he gestured a no with his hands. "You have dated a few ladies. I mean, there has been Tolani, Ify, Sarai, Akosua, Naima....." "Alright now mother...." Jay interrupted laughing. "Well, I am just trying to figure out why this one is different." Elena chuckled. "She is! She is just... I can't explain it." He responded smiling at the thought of Leya. Elena caught his look, "So, when do I meet this lady who gives you peace then?" she asked sipping on her drink. "At the right time and Amara needs to stop running to you every time we have a tiff. Does she not even have a mother for goodness sake? Why is she always running to mine?" Jay asked raising his voice. His mum smiled, sipping on her drink.

****

"No, no, noooo" Leya stressed, as she took a shower. Jay had invited her to his family's annual barbeque. He had not been thrice in a row and absolutely hated it! However, for some strange reason, he really wanted to go with Leya this year. Her presence made him feel alive, he truly enjoyed having her around him. Brushing his teeth, bare chested, towel round his waist, he walked over to Leya in the shower. "C'mon" Jay pleaded, the toothbrush still in his mouth, watching her naked body as the rhythm of the shower washed over her beautiful soft curves, and slickly full, highly plump breast. She was beautiful in every sense of the word! "I'm not going" she reiterated, wiping the water off her face. "C'mon, it's a chance to meet my family." "Jay, I'm not going to your family barbeque" she persisted. He washed his mouth and came round to prop his side on the shower door. "Why not?" He asked. "You want all these rich, rich people, to look at me and sniff me like a dog? No, thank you" she said turning off the shower. Leya picked up her towel, wrapping it around her chest and stepped out. "No one's going to sniff you like a dog" he told her, looking at her admiringly. "You know what I mean" she responded. "You don't like me, you this man" she continued, "You want me to go so they can dissect me and ask all kinds of questions I won't be able to answer." Jay walked behind her, turning her towards him, "You think I'll let that happen to you?" He asked looking at her with the intense gaze he gave her when he meant what he said. "I don't know Jay" she said, looking at him deflated. "I'd normally not go to these family gatherings myself but your company gives me an inexplicable comfort. I feel I can do anything with you around me." He looked at her body, loosening the towel and holding each ends with his hands. "Now," he said looking at her seductively, "Did you wash up well?" Smiling, she replied shyly, "Um huh." "Hmmmm" he said, assessing her naked body. "Think I might have to check for myself." "Leave me jor" she responded, taking the towel edges from him in playful aggression and wrapping it back on her chest. As she turned to walk away, he crept up behind her slowly, taking her unawares. She let out a playful scream when he carried her towards the bedroom and shut the door with his leg.

After Jay had successfully persuaded Leya into going for the barbecue, she needed some moral support, some sort of convincing and who better to call than her mother hen. After all, Bunmi had never been to visit her at the new home since she moved in with Jay. As Bunmi entered the house, she looked around in sheer shock and excitement screaming, "Leyaaaaaa. Hah! So this is how you have just left me in face me I face you house, wey if shit catch you when someone dey toilet, na to shit for rubber ni o" she said still looking around. Bunmi could not contain her excitement as she intentionally dropped her body onto the sofa and in a dreamy state began to talk, "Imagine say na me get this house. I go just enter" she got up mimicking the role of a madam. "I go just waka like this. Come see you for here, come be like, hellowww, how can I help you," mimicking a foreign accent. Leya giggled! "I go come be like, oh sit, sit." gesturing to Leya. "I go now come call my house girl. Charity, charittyyyyy" Leya burst into laughter, "Leave this Charity girl alone now." "How will I leave her? That pest! Sometimes I just want to break her into two sef" Bunmi replied sitting down again. She grabbed a pillow and threw it at Leya, "So, have you guys finally done the diddy?" Leya smiled sheepishly and nodded! Bunmi began to hype her friend, "Baby girl of life! How was it? Give me gist jor." Coyly, Leya said to her, "It was amazing Bunmi, I have nev......" All the while looking at her suspiciously, Bunmi cut in, "You kissed him didn't you?" Leya could not respond. "You kissed the malafacka" Bunmi shouted chuckling and playfully hitting Leya. "O' ti shele" Bunmi exclaimed in Yoruba before saying it again in English, "It has happened oo." "It's not like that" Leya interrupted. "The plan was not to fall in love o Leya mi. Na to chop clean mouth. These people are not on our level" Bunmi reminded her worryingly. "Now he wants me to go to a family barbecue with him." "Family kini? Both of you are just falling on your own" she laughed. "I don't want to go Bunmi" Leya blurted out, a worried look on her face. "What if someone recognises me?" "Sis mi" Bunmi assured her, "These ones are not our kind of customers. No be those idiots wey dey give us 2k, 3k o. You no go find these kain people for our area now. So feel free abeg." "I should go?" Leya asked, looking surprised. "Baby girl, spread your wings and flyyyyy. Now, what is in this you rich people your fridge, let me cool myself" as she walked towards the kitchen with Leya following behind. Bunmi screamed as she entered the kitchen, "See person kitchen ooooo!"

"Family is not an important thing, it's everything" – Michael J Fox

Jay and Leya had arrived at his parents' home. She was as nervous as a hare – having never been to anyone's party before. The only party she knew were the ones the bars threw, filled with drunken men throwing up all over her. She had made the effort to look good at least, dressed in a denim mini smock dress with gold buttons at the front and her converse all-star trainers, her luscious curls falling over her shoulder in a side part. She got out of the car gripping the door handle. "You'll be fine" Jay said holding her by the shoulder in a reassuring manner. "Easy for you to say. Your mum is in there, along with all these gossip aunties waiting for food to feast on" she pointed towards the house. "You look stunning, let go" as he tried to move her hand from the door handle. "No!" Leya said, firmly gripping the door handle. A voice interrupted them, "Heyyyy, look who we have here" Fred, Jay's cousin and best friend said walking over to them and giving Jay a big hug. He had grown up with Jay when his parents got divorced at a very young age, leaving Elena to fill in the role of mum in his life. Except for the few times when he visited his own mother who lived in South Africa with her new family. Most times, he felt like an outsider when he was with his other family and even though his mum showered him with a lot of love and

80

affection, he still preferred being home with his paternal aunt. "My man!" Jay said, happy to see each other. Fred looked over Jay speechless. "Who's this beauty?" He asked, walking over to Leya. Jay laughed, "My girl, Leya." His words took Leya aback as she stared at him in shock. *His girl*, she thought to herself, a smile almost forming at the corners of her mouth. Were she not a nervous wreck at the moment, she would have grabbed her man and kissed him - her man! *It felt good to think that*, she thought. "Your girl hah" Fred said as he hugged Leya. "Nice to meet you. The name's Fred. Gosh, you are beautiful" he said looking her up and down, admiringly. "Okay now" Jay interrupted trying to separate them, Fred laughed. "A massive step up from you know who," Fred whispered quietly to Jay who chuckled! "Alright guys, let's go in. The others are dying to see you Jay. You don't like these family barbecues" Fred playfully nudged him. "It's just long maaan. And everyone asking the million dollar question," "When are you getting married?" They both said simultaneously and laughed. He beckoned to Leya, who held on to Jay's arm as though her life depended on it. Fred took the lead as Jay walked behind with Leya, kissing her temple and whispering, "You'll be fine."

The Family barbecue was in full session when they walked in! Music on blast, the cocktail bar was surrounded by some family members engaged in conversations full of laughter. Whilst others preferred to hang around the barbecue area, munching on the tasty meat straight off the grill as the younger ones showed off their swim skills in the pool. Everyone was clearly having a good time. Whilst some looked like they were dressed for a gala event, others were very casual which made Leya feel a bit at ease. This was the thing Jay hated about his circle – the need for everyone to try and out do the other by showing off their latest designer purchase just to prove a point. Fred shouted out! "Hey everyone, look who we have here!" They turned and yelled in excitement as they saw Jay, walking over to hug him. The little ones were clearly ecstatic to see Jay as they rushed to hug him in their wetsuits. Elena sat all the while, silently watching from a distance. Her gaze particularly on Leya. "Uncle T!" Jay exclaimed excitedly at a middle aged man with bald head and a full grey beard. He walked over wearing a black apron and a spatula in his hand, giving Jay a big hug. "My boyyyyy" he said looking at Jay and hugging him again. Leya looked around nervously. Uncle Tyrone was Fred's dad, Elena's brother. He was the life and soul of the party, a bit of a Casanova with his devilish good looks! There was absolutely no fun without Uncle T as he was affectionately called. "How are you?" Uncle T asked smiling. "Very well" Jay responded. Uncle T noticed Leya, "What an absolutely gorgeous girl you got here" he said smiling at Leya. Jay looked at her, "Meet Leya, Uncle T." "An absolute pleasure" he replied, taking her hand and kissing it. "You got my nephew to come to our family barbecue? Lady, I owe you one tasty grilled chicken." Jay and Leya laughed. "We have lots on the grill though. I hope you guys are hungry" said Uncle T. "Where's mum?" Jay asked. "Over there," Uncle T pointed to Elena sitting on the patio, wearing a sun hat, her favourite Prada sunglasses, and an off shoulder bejewelled maxi dress. "I'll be back" he smiled at Uncle T and held Leya's hand as they walked over to his mum. "You seem to be doing well so far" he told her. "Hah, I'm not o! It's like I want to pee sef" she responded. He laughed just as they got to his mum. "Mum" he bowed, his fingers almost touching the ground as a sign of respect and in line with their culture, before giving her a kiss. She looked at Leya and said to her, "Whatever you're doing, it's a great cus this son of mine never comes for the family barbecue." Leya smiled, shyly tucking

83

further into Jay's arm. "And your name is?" Elena asked. "Leya" she responded. "Leya. Quite an unusual name. Lovely all the same," Elena said to Leya who responded with a shy "Thank you." "Sit" she gestured to them. They sat down, Leya shifted uncomfortably, playing with her fingers. There was something about Jay's mum that she could not put a finger on. Her eyes were powerful, that explained where Jay got his intense gaze from. She looked like a woman not to be reckoned with. Elena stared at her, "So, what is it you do and how did you two meet? Spill the tea" She asked smiling. Leya shifted uncomfortably in her chair once again. As she cleared her throat to speak, Jay quickly cut in and said to his mum. "She's a student." "I see.....and what are you studying?" Elena continued. "Human anatomy" Leya answered. Jay almost burst out in laughter, only controlling himself when his mum looked at him. "Something funny?" Elena asked. "Nah, no mum" he answered, trying so hard not to laugh. His mum turned back to Leya, "I do not know what's tickling my son but you can talk to me. What about your parents?" And at that moment, saved by the bell, Uncle T walked over to Leya moving his hips and upper body in the funniest dance moves. "Leya, come dance with me beautiful" he stretched his hand to her. Leya hesitated, looking at Jay who nodded his head convincing her to go with him. She got up and went with Uncle T as they joined the others on the dance floor doing the electric slide. Jay smiled, sipping his drink as he watched her affectionately. Elena looked at her son and then turned to look at Leya who was giggling whilst watching Uncle T's funny moves to the electric slide dance. "Amara......" his mum began as they watched the family members on the dance floor, "No mum, not today please" Jay pleaded. "I didn't say anything" Elena replied. "Yes you did" Jay said, his gaze still on Leya who caught his stare and made a funny face at him winking, he giggled and winked back! "Do you even know this girl?" Elena asked concerned, following Jay's gaze. "We are getting to know each other" he responded. "She does seem like a lovely girl, but you're heir to a large corporation my lovely" reaching out to hold his hand. "Who you end up with as a life partner is very important. Not just for you, but the family and business as a whole." Jay looked at his mum, stood up, kissed her cheek and said, "You're right! But today, I just want to have a good time." He bent to pick up his drink, "Going to catch up with the others, love you." He said to his mum looking on at him as he walked away.

85

There was truly something about this girl Leya, Elena thought to herself as she looked out the window at her son and the girl who had obviously captured his heart. They were clearly into each other, laughing their heads off at whatever it was they were talking about. Leya intrigued her! Who was she? At that moment, Fred walked up to Elena still looking out the window. He looked out at them too and said calmly, "Looks like Jay's caught the love bug. I mean, she's beautiful." "It's not about beauty" Elena responded, her attention on them. "There's something about her that fascinates me," Elena continued. Fred replied, "True! Just wondering where Jay met her? Never seen her in our circle but for some reason, she does look familiar, just not sure where." "Hmm, I see!" Elena said quietly, eyes still fixed on Jay and Leya.

7

"The way I see it, if you want the rainbow, you gotta put up with the rain" – Dolly Parton

Thursday nights were for the Gym. Jay and Fred along with two of their friends, Tayo and Chuks met regularly catching up amidst a good work out session. Jay was working out of town, hence the three decided to engage in their weekly routine without him. "Yo mehnn, I missed the all great Daniels family barbecue" Tayo metioned. "Indeed you did. Jay showed up" Fred called out as he ran on the treadmill. "No wayyy! He absolutely hates it" Tayo exclaimed laughing. "Yeah I know but he came with this gorgeous girl and I guess it's pretty serious if he actually brought her to the gathering" Fred continued, wiping sweat off his face with the towel on his shoulder. "What? A girl? He brought a girl to the barbecue? Well, thanks to my flight, I've missed out on the opportunity to take a dig at him and ask the infamous question" as Fred and Tayo said simultaneously laughing, "When are you getting married?" "On a serious note though, I'd take this new chic over Amara. Girl is such a bitch" Fred said. Tayo laughed, "Amara and her attitude can fill a whole book dude. This girl....." Tayo said, "Leya?" Fred answered. "What? Her name is Leya?" Tayo asked. "Yeah, why?" "Name sounds familiar" Tayo responded as he walked over to pick some weights. " I thought so too" Fred confirmed. "Chuks!" Tayo called out! Chuks walked over, "Sup?" He asked. "Does the name Leya sound familiar" Tayo asked. "Why?" Chuks asked. "There's this girl Jay brought to the barbecue called Leya and we both thought her name sounded familiar" Fred said. Chuks laughed, "We heard about this prostitute, call girl, whatever you want to call it, who never kisses or gives head. Came up in a conversation at happy hour a few months ago when we got tipsy and horny, looking for a girl to give us a good time." "Ahhhhhh" Fred and Tayo both responded, remembering why the name was familiar. "Well, I guess there can't be only one Leya in the world" Fred said. "True" Tayo replied. "Chuks knows her though," Tayo continued. "Remember when I told you, dude got drunk. Ended up downtown, met the babe who immediately gave him her rules." "Ashawo on another level" Chuks laughed. "I was like, what the fuck! I just want some head and you're giving all these do's and don'ts. I told her to get out of my car." "Did she change her mind?" Fred asked. "Change her mind!" Chuks repeated. "Babe just calmly opened the door and stepped out." They burst out laughing. "Speaking of Jay's Leya, I think she's in the video I captured at the bbq." He reached out into his trouser pocket and they all gathered to watch. Chuks shouted in astonishment, "Leya!" Fred looked at Tayo and then at Chuks and muttered, "Oh shit!"

It had been such an unwelcomed revelation. Fred could not believe a girl as beautiful and level headed as Leya was a prostitute. Her look was warm and welcoming, almost innocent. It had bothered him all night on the way back home. He knew he had to speak to Jay before his aunty found out.

****

Jay stood, looking out the office window, taking in the scenery from his 5th floor office, his back to Fred. "You knew?" Fred asked surprised. "Yes" he turned to look at Fred. "Well, initially, I didn't. Then I found out." "What is wrong with you man" Fred asked confused. "Do you have any idea what this means at all? And God help you if Aunty E finds out." Jay paced up and down his office, sleeves rolled up to his arms, hands in his pocket. "I know Fred, I know" he said taking his left hand out of his pocket rubbing his head and his beard. "She's an amazing girl" Jay said. Fred looked at him in a frown! "I mean, granted, she has a past..." "Past?" Fred cut in. "Dude, her past was only a few months ago. She's stunning and all but c'mon now, c'mon" Fred exclaimed! Jay sat down whilst Fred sat across the table from him. "This is serious man! Of all the women you've met Jay. Look, I was at the gym, talking about the barbecue and you showing up with this gorgeous girl. Her name comes up, the guys thought it sounded familiar, rest is history. I even bloody said I'd take Leya over Amara any day with her bitch ass attitude, but dude you know what this means? It means everywhere you go, people know your woman to be the famous call girl with her I don't suck dick catchphrase" Fred said to Jay with a look of worry on his face.

"Maaan, this is major! May-jor," Fred stressed, exasperated as he fell back into his seat, his hands raised above his head in contemplation. "Besides, how do you know she's not only in for the money? Remember, she's been with a few men to know the games of the trade. You think she doesn't know what she's doing?" He asked. "I mean, look at you. Single, tall, dark, handsome with a whole lot of money to spend. I tell you man, these hoes aint loyal." Jay looked at him, concern written all over his face.

Jay had driven home in silence! He had been drowned in Leya's wit, personality and sultry look the first time they met that he had not really thought this through. He felt something different for this girl, she was like no other woman he had dated. It was not just about the strong intimacy they shared, which he enjoyed. The universe had given his soul a twin and it reflected each day and night they spent together. However Fred was right about the consequences of his action, the blog headlines and the unnecessary media frenzy! He was torn between the devil and the blue sea. Indeed a part of him was willing to fight for this and face the consequences and a part of him was worried about putting his family in the limelight. A situation they had prevented for many years. He sat in his car for a few seconds when he arrived home before picking up his laptop bag and getting out. Leya ran up to hug and kiss him the moment he walked through the door. She noticed his stiff response, "Are you okay?" she asked concerned, taking his blazer and laptop bag from him. "Yeah, good. Just need a rest" he said "Bad day at the office?" "You could say that" he responded. She looked at him for a few minutes and then gently said, "Your family found out about me didn't they?" He looked at her surprised. This is what he meant by finding his twin! How is it she could read his mind he wondered? "What makes you think that?" He asked. "Nothing" she responded. He sat on the sofa. "Who knows?" She asked, standing over him, a look of worry on her face. "Does it matter? It makes no difference" he responded abrasively. "I knew this was going to happen the moment I decided to go to that nonsense barbecue with you." "Nonsense?" Jay asked, looking at her and then standing up, "Did you say Nonsense?" "Yes, nonsense! Silly rich people who think they're better than everyone else" Leya responded, her voice raised. "Well, those people work hard for their money" Jay retorted. "What's that supposed to mean?" she asked angrily. "People like you....." "People like me?" She interrupted angrily. "Yes, people like you. Some of you ladies always wanting the cheap way out without having to actually work for it!" Jay responded, more frustrated than angry. "Look Jay, I don't know or care about what has been said to you but don't come here taking your anger out on me. Ah ah! What is it? You knew who I was before you asked me to come and live with you," her speech crackled and began to get emotional. "I mean, what happened to hustling for jobs like other girls with a bit of decency" he continued, unaware of the tears that started to trickle down her face. She quickly wiped it! "Fuck you Jay, fuck you" she retorted! "How lady like!" Jay sneered. "I may be a prostitute but I have morals okay." Leya continued as another tear fell down. Jay let out a sarcastic laugh, "Morals? What? Because you don't kiss or suck dick? That makes you better than the others? At the end of the day, it is what it is, you're a...." "Prostitute" Leya finished off his statement. He looked at her, a feeling of regret began to wash over his face. "Hoe, ashawo, runs girl, commercial sex worker, fucking whore. Are those enough words to describe me?" Leya asked, her voice broken, as she turned to walk upstairs. Jay watched as she left. Pacing about, he hit the wall with his fist muttering to himself, "You idiot." Few moments later, Leya came downstairs with the suitcase she moved in with and gently walked past Jay trying so hard to fight the tears defeating her as they fell down her eyes. "Where are you going" he asked. She ignored him but then suddenly turned to him spontaneously, "You know, all along, I knew this was too good to be true anyway. The rich boy, their unspoken rules and the call girl from the hood." She let out a short emotional laugh amidst the tears now freely flowing. "I knew this was a dream, a fantasy, but I loved living this fantasy. It is the only good thing I have ever had." She broke down completely in tears. Jay moved to hold her but she flinched from his touch. He held back! "I'm a rose Jay! I'm just a rose with many thorns but I know, I know I'm......" She stopped, hesitated and then said to him, "Good bye" as she opened the door and stepped out. Jay paced up and down the house like a man waiting to hear some kind of news! Why did he have to take out his frustration on her? Goodness! He had never seen her this way before, she looked broken and vulnerable. There was a sudden innocence about her that made broken look so beautiful. He ran out the house after her!

He scanned the area, she couldn't have gone far. It was a high brow residential area and there were no taxis or motorcycle around. Leya walked by the road dragging her suitcase, the wheels making a crackling sound. She fought hard to suppress the tears, sniffing loudly when she heard her name, "Leya, Leyaaaa." She turned to see Jay and kept walking, ignoring him. His voice louder, he cried out, "Please stop, please." Leya stopped walking. He ran to catch up with her, a little out of breath. "I'm sorry" he whispered. "All that was so unnecessary, I shouldn't have said the things I said. I'm sorry" he continued, wiping the tears from her eyes. She looked away as he continued, "Fred found out about you from the guys at the gym and I guess I got so worked up after he came to my office with a long lecture. I'm so stupid to have taken it out on you. I'm such an asshole" he muttered to himself. "Come back! Please." He said, stretching his hand to take her suitcase away from her. Leya looked down at her feet, the tears uncontrollable. He lifted her chin and wiped her face with his shirt. Putting his arm around her, they walked back to the house in silence.

"All the adversity I've had in my life, all my troubles and obstacles have strengthened me...You may not realise it when it happens, but a kick in the teeth may be the best thing in the world for you" – Walt Disney

8

"When you meet someone for the first time, that's not the whole book. That's just the first page" – Brody Dalle

It had been an eventful night – their first argument! They had returned to the house quietly and Jay had taken her suitcase back upstairs. He returned to find her sitting cross legged on the sofa, her arms wrapped around herself. She looked different, almost childlike! He walked over to her, sitting down he took her in his arms, tracing her arm with his fingers. "You want me to get you anything?" He asked, she nodded her head in silence. Resting in his arms quietly for what felt like forever, suddenly she began to speak.

"....I was left in front of the gate of an orphanage a few months old with nothing but a strange inscription under my left arm." Jay raised his head to look at the mark and touched it, as Leya continued. "I spent my growing years there and it was okay. I mean, there were no birthdays or special moments, but we had food to eat and shelter. I had just turned twelve when one of the care workers started to take a particular liking to me. I liked that for once, someone actually liked me and gave me some form of attention. He would buy me little things like biscuit, yogurt" she giggled, "and tell me how beautiful I was. It made me feel so special. One day, he asked me to come see him that he had gotten me some nice clothes and that pretty girls deserved good things. I remember standing in the mirror, making my hair, powdering my face with white powder. Maybe I was going to get even more goodies if he saw me looking more beautiful. I went to see him, in a building just in the corner of the compound. It was so hidden, one would not notice any body going and coming out of that place. I felt it strange that he would ask me to come there because normally, he would give me the gifts in the office in the presence of the other staff. I brushed the thought away and knocked on the door. He answered, I went in. He started praising me as usual and told me to sit down. I was smiling and excited about my gift. He came to sit next to me, looked at me and said "You're a beautiful girl" I smiled. He continued, "I see your breast has developed and your body has shaped up well." I felt uncomfortable as he stretched his arms to touch my small breast. I shifted away from him, he moved closer. I asked him about my gift. "Oh, your gift, I'll give it to you. I want us to talk first," the idiot said. I looked at him confused, like, what were we going to talk about? I was there for my gift, which one was talking. He put his arms around me and asked if I had ever been with a man, I shook my head. I didn't know where this was going. He said I was lying, that those small small boys have been touching me haven't they? I said no sir, no one has touched me before. "You're a virgin then," he responded with an excitement on his face that seemed so strange. Everything was just strange to me. Suddenly, almost like he had been possessed, the man held me firmly, I tried to move his arm but he was too strong for me. I started to beg him to leave me and I didn't want his present anymore. By this time he had torn my pant, I started to cry, begging him to let me go. He used one hand to cover my mouth, I bit his palm so hard, he slapped me, knocking me off the bed. He grabbed me and warned that I keep my mouth shut else he'll kill me and no one will ever find out. He pushed me on to the bed, and when he penetrated me, I screamed! The most excruciating pain I had ever felt. Like my flesh was tearing apart" Jay looked at her, sadness in his eyes and put his head on her shoulder. "I'm so sorry" he said, kissing her shoulder gently. Leya continued, "After, I lay there with blood all over my crotch, silent, confused and a burning pain down there. He came to sit next to me, apologising that he could not resist me, that he loved me and this will never happen again. He brought me water and a tablet to drink saying it'll make me feel better. Now I realise, each time he gave me this tablet, it was to prevent conception. He told me to promise not to tell anyone and that this was going to be our little secret. I just sat there numb. Numb from the pain, the shock. Did the rape stop?" She laughed. "No! He would find any opportunity to force himself on me. When I tried to scream, he would put me in a choke hold position and have his way with me. Sometimes I passed out, he was like an animal when he was on me. I couldn't take it anymore, so one day, I lied to the gateman that Aunty Sally, the head in charge had sent me to get her clothes from the tailor. The children were not allowed out without adult supervision and I remember him looking at me suspiciously but he opened the gate after a while. I ran with nothing on me but the locket from my birth mother hidden in my chest. Here I was, living rough on the streets, begging to eat. There was a school in the area that had no wall and I remember sneaking up to the class window to learn as the teacher taught the class. I used a stick and the sand on the ground as my pen and paper" she let out a painful laugh. "When I turned 16, I saw an advert for a housemaid. I applied lying to the madam I was 18, she believed me! That woman was very nice to me, God bless her wherever she is." Jay raised his head to look at Leya, "Why? What happened to her?" he asked. Leya continued with a sad smile, "We lived well together until one day, I was home alone and her husband came. It was odd that he was home earlier than usual. I greeted him and asked if he was okay as he was home early and I had not started to make the evening meal. He smiled gently at me and said he had a slight headache and wanted to go and rest. I asked if he wanted me to get him some medicine and he looked at me for a few seconds without saying a word. It made me feel a bit uncomfortable but it seemed harmless. He asked if I could bring him some paracetamol and water, I nodded." Jay sat up on the sofa and sighed, rubbing his head in his hands as Leya continued to tell her story, still cross legged as she always sat. "So, I took the medicine to him. He was lying down, eyes closed. I tapped him, he opened his eyes and took the tablet from me and the water, drinking it. I turned to leave and he held my hand. I remember looking at him and then at my hand. He said he was lonely, I should keep him company. Ah! Which company again? I started to have flash backs from the orphanage and aggressively pushed his hand away. That was my mistake! The man stood up and pushed me so hard on the bed ehnn. I started to scream and struggle with him, he punched me so hard in the face and said, "I pay your wages and you are here in this house to offer a service, any kind of service I require." This was the most vicious of rape, he hit me so bad because I struggled with him. Later that evening when his wife came home, my eyes and face were swollen and I had been crying. I tried to hide the bruises on my face with her make up. She looked at me and asked if I was alright. I told her I had just received a message from the village that my mother had died. She felt so bad and asked if I wanted some time to go back to the village and I said yes. I remember going to bed that night with a knife under my pillow in case her husband tried to come and have his way with me. I didn't care if I killed him, after all, I had nothing to lose. He did not come. In the morning, his wife came to see me, gave me 20,000 naira and told me to go to the village as we discussed, to sort out funeral arrangements. I looked at her and for the first time in my life, I wished I really did have a mother. The emotions came pouring out as I hugged her so hard, so hard, thanking her for her kindness. She smiled and gave me a week to return. I never did!

"I was back on the streets again" Leya chuckled at the memory. I would roam the area during the day, washing plates in the local bars, selling scraps and broken bottles and sometimes stealing. When it was night time, I would wait for this lady who owned a hair shop in the area to close for the night so I could put my wrapper on the floor in front of her shop and sleep. After weeks of sleeping rough, the don of the area who had started taken a liking to me came to where I lay, my eyes were closed. I felt someone try to pull my cloth off my legs and I opened my eyes. I asked what he was trying to do and he said he wanted to come and gist. This was all too familiar abeg. I asked him what gist he wanted to gist at 11pm. He laughed and said I'm a small girl, I need to shine my eyes and understand. Oh, I understood! I understood so well. He started to get closer to me, touching my thighs and trying to get his hands up to my pant, telling me he was going to protect me and people in the area will fear me if I became his woman. I looked at the rugged, smelling piece of shit before me and all the years of anger just came flooding in. Recently I had bought a knife to protect myself and I don't know when I ran the knife straight into his stomach, not once, not twice, I can't even remember how many times until his guts spilled out. When I realised what I had done, I ran, My God I ran! I knew I had stabbed the chief cultist in the area and if his people found me, they would lynch me! I kept running until I got to the bus station. Met a night driver and when he saw me panting, bloodied and so scared, he thought I had run away from kidnappers or ritual killers. I begged him to save my life, kept telling him to save me, the man looked at me and asked how he could save me, scanning his eyes around to check who was after me. I asked if he was travelling the night and he said yes. I asked if I could board his bus, he did not say a word but just led me to the bus and gave me a seat. No ticket, nothing. God bless that man!" Leya wiped tears from her eyes as Jay looked on so helpless, holding one of her hands and covering it with his. Leya continued, "I sat on that bus and woke up in Lagos. I came to Lagos with nothing but the blood stained dress I was wearing and some change in my pocket. Each job I tried to apply for was the same old story of my life – sex before work! One day, I decided if that was the case, then so be it. After all, sex meant nothing to me, it was not emotional, and it was not even pleasurable. I had experienced it a time too many to know it was absolutely nothing when people talked about sex being this and that. I told myself I wasn't going to kiss my customer or engage in any other sexual activity. My business was for only down there, you do, pay me and go, that's it! The first night I walked the streets, a regular worker tried to get into a fight with me and that's when I met Bunmi" Leya smiled. "Bunmi fought for me like she knew me and took me in to live with her at....." "G house" Jay interrupted smiling. Leya giggled, "Yes, G house! A stranger she had never met before, she became like a mother and a sister all in one. Bunmi talked me through the sex trade, what to do and what not to do. I remember the first night I slept with a customer, I came back and scrubbed my body so bad that I heard Bunmi asking if I had craw craw" Leya said laughing with sadness written all over her face. "I walked the streets until I met you. You showed me unconditional love and that sex also was pleasurable. That there was actually something called love making and one could have multiple orgasms at a go." Jay reached out to her, cupping her face in his hands as he kissed her passionately. His emotions letting go and a deep stirring within him, he looked into her eyes and said to her, "I'm going to protect you, love you, with my heart and my body. From the moment I met you, I knew there was more to you than the girl in her mini skirt and see through top" he teased. She playfully hit his arm giggling. They gazed into each other's eyes in silence, "You're all I've ever wanted Miss Leya" Jay whispered to her as he planted his lips on hers. Leya closed her eyes savouring his kiss!

"It's only through stepping into the pain that we can finally free ourselves from the pain" – Debra L Reble PhD

9

"Three things cannot be long hidden: the sun, the moon and the truth" - Buddha

Leya had felt relief after reliving the memories of her past! She never thought she would share this with anyone else but Bunmi, however she had opened up to Jay! He had suddenly become so protective of her since finding out that she playfully called him her daddy sometimes, but she loved it! The feeling of loving and being loved – she was happy!

Bunmi had come over to visit and was sitting with Leya in the Patio having a good laugh as they always did. Bunmi's face turned serious looking at Leya, "I'm glad you told him baby girl, but I sha don't know how this you people your love is going to be o because ice and fire no dey mix ra ra. But as he loves you, you people can overcome anything." "Just taking it one day at a time" Leya said. "That's all you can do" Bunmi responded as Leya's phone rang. She stared at it, smiled and picked up, "Hey beautiful," Jay said, his rich deep voice over the phone. "Hey" Leya responded smiling. "You okay? Been thinking about you. Gosh, you're all I think about actually," he laughed. Leya blushed as Bunmi stared at her, shaking her head at Leya's demeanour. "I've been thinking. How would you like to go back to school?" Jay asked. Leya covered her mouth with her hands in shock before she exclaimed in excitement, "Oh my God. Oh my God, yes, yes please," Jay laughed! "Good then, we'll talk about this when I get home" he said. "Got to run into a meeting, speak later." Hanging up, he looked at his phone for a few seconds, a smile plastered all over his face, before putting it in his pocket and walking out of his office. "What was that about?" Bunmi asked wondering. Leya crip walked towards Bunmi playfully, "Welllll, he wants me to go back to school." "Ah ah, I go love oooooo" Bunmi shouted, when suddenly the gate opened and a black Mercedes drove in. Parking a few metres away from Bunmi and Leya, Amara stepped out of the car in her white Balmain blazer with gold buttons over a white vest tucked into a pair of jeans and red heels. She had a shorter wig this time, a pixie cut. Clutching her LV bag under her arm, she walked towards them. Bunmi whispered to Leya, "Na the girl be dis?" Leya nodded and responded, looking straight at Amara, "I have this one's time today, let her come." Amara got to their spot and blurted out, "Jay here?" "They did not teach you how to greet where you're coming from abi?" Bunmi said to her. Amara ignored her and looked at Leya, "Is Jay in?" "Does it look like he's in?" Leya asked "No need for the catty attitude, I'm here to see my man. You answer yes or no, simple." Leya looked at Bunmi and they burst out in laughter. "See this one o" Bunmi said gesturing her hand at Amara. "Your man. You don't have man in this house o aunty." "Don't call me aunty" Amara shouted at Bunmi, interrupting her. "If I call you aunty nko? You be like person aunty now. I said you don't have any man in this house, now turn, enter your motor and drive awayyyyy." Bunmi shouted, moving towards her. "I will not be humiliated by two uncouth, uneducated, locals" Amara responded. Leya got up, "Get out!" she gestured to Amara, "Get out before I do what I don't want to do" she shouted. "You're threatening me?" Amara laughed,

"You're going to regret this" she said as she walked away to her car. "Regret what?" Bunmi asked, "Abeg gooooo" she continued, as they watched Amara get into her car and drive off angrily. Leya shouted out at the gateman who ran over to them in a panic. "Idris, if you ever, ever let that woman into this house again ehnn" Leya warned. "Sorry madam, no be say na anything o. But as she be former madam I come think say she no be stranger," he said apologetically. "I no go try am again, abeg no vex" still apologetic as he walked away to his base.

****

Leya had been excited about enrolling in school. Jay had pulled some strings and talks were in place for her to take the entrance exams to study business management. She had to learn the basics first and spent her day time at the library and her evenings on the computer at home. Jay could not have been more proud! She had committed herself to hours of studying that she had started to feel hunger pangs. Walking to the kitchen to fix something for herself, she heard the doorbell ring. Ignoring, she went to the kitchen, opening the cupboard, taking out a packet of noodles and emptying the contents in a bowl. The doorbell rang again!

Leya wondered who that might be as she walked to the front door holding a kitchen napkin and cleaning her hands. As she opened the door, she was taken aback, shocked to see Elena standing there. "H-he-hello ma" she greeted Elena. Elena walked into the house like a queen in full regalia. There was something powerful about her, she had a distinctive force of command about her. Looking around, she turned to look at Leya, "Hello" she smiled. "J-Jay is not here" Leya stuttered! "I know" she answered, sitting down. "Sit" she gestured at a nervous Leya who almost lost her balance trying to sit down. Elena looked at Leya as she nervously tucked her hands between her legs. "Do you love my son" She asked. The question caught Leya off guard who looked at her confused. "Err, ermmm" she replied, "Not an immediate answer I see." Elena interrupted! "No, Yes, I mean...." Elena cut in again, "Do you think love is enough?" She asked Leya. "Sorry?" Leya asked, more confused at the unfolding drama before her. What was this? Why was she asking her all these questions? Leya's mind raced. "Do you think love is enough? I mean, an eligible bachelor, heir to an empire and extremely hardworking, meets a woman, a woman he is clearly smitten by" Elena said looking at Leya, "and throws caution to the wind." "I,

I don't get what you mean Ma" Leya said nervously. Elena stared at her in silence, Leya got up! "Ca, can I get you a drink" she asked. "Yes of course, by all means" Elena replied smiling at Leya. Leya walked hurriedly to the fridge, taking nervous deep breaths, before picking a glass and a bottle to Elena. As she was about to pour the drink, Elena continued, "So, what was it you said you studied again at University?" "Ermmm, errr, human anatomy Ma" She stuttered, as she handed the drink to Elena. Elena let out a short laugh, "I didn't know this was the fancy word for prostitution these days" she said. Leya almost dropped the bottle and caught it quickly, her hands trembling! "I think you should sit before you fall" Elena told her, gesturing to a chair. Leya sat with her head bowed. Elena looked at her, smiled and continued, "I mean, look at it this way. A politician is vying for office, words get out that his wife has been around the block, with many men testifying to encounters with her. Do you know how huge a scandal that will cause?" Leya nodded. "You see, I understand that one can find love in the craziest places but love my darling, is never enough! The first day I met you, I thought and still think you're a gorgeous girl, but you intrigued me. To protect the interest of my son and my household, I wanted to know more.

More about this girl who could actually get my son to attend a family barbecue which he absolutely detests" Elena chuckled. "Imagine my disappointment finding out you're a call girl, and quite famous for certain reasons I understand" she said, picking up a magazine, flipping through and pretending to read. Leya sat as still as a statue while Elena continued to speak. "Your life is riddled with tales of men you have sold your body to. Pretty girls who do not want to work hard to make something for themselves but would rather lay on their backs and spread their legs. For how much exactly?" she asked Leya who tried to hold back the tears. She had made some poor decisions in her life and it was coming back to haunt her. Elena stood up, "You see, it has taken us forty odd years to build a global empire. 40 years with no tales of scandals whatsoever. I am not going to sit down, fold my arms and watch my son, my only child throw caution to the wind" she spoke sternly as she picked up her handbag. "Speaking about love, I do not think you love my son, you would have wanted the best for him. For you see, some people are meant only to stay in your heart, but not in your life." She looked at Leya for a few seconds, noticing the tears. "Do I hate you? No, not at all. In a very strange way, you remind me of me, but I'll be honest with you, no mother would sit back and watch her child put their hands in fire." She headed towards the door and turned for a brief second to look at Leya sitting face down, hands between her laps and walked out.

"At the end of the day, you can either focus on what's tearing you apart or what's keeping you together" – *Anonymous*

"A whore! Jason Olugbenga Daniels. You're dating a prostitute. Has it gotten to this?" Elena asked, her voice raised. "Is this why you felt the need to come over and put her down more than she already is?" Jay asked his mum angrily "You have to understand...." "...Understand" she echoed, interrupting him. "Understand that my only child, my son has decided to ultimately cohabit with a call girl" She shouted. "Hah! Gbenga, Gbenga mi" his mum spoke softly, walking over to touch his face. "I am sick and tired of Amara always coming to report my business to you" he said to his mother. "Amara did the right thing coming to tell me what recently happened when she came over to see you. She met your absence but rather had a chance ratchet encounter with your call girl and a friend. You see, her reputation will always follow her okoh mi *meaning my husband, which was an endearment term in their Yoruba language*. Is this what you want?" Elena asked concerned. "I wish you understood the kind of peace she gives me" Jay said, walking over to sit down. "Peace" his mum repeated his word following him to sit on the sofa. "Peace? So the Karma Sutra positions she has acquired skills in over the years is your own definition of peace abi?" she asked. "Nooo, no!" Jay exclaimed, stressing on his words. "It's not even about the sex. Granted, the sex is great. It's amazing but she........hold on, why am I even discussing my sex life with you right now" he replied. His mum chuckled looking at him, and ever so calmly said to her son, "They say, what the elders see whilst sitting down, the young ones standing on their toes cannot see." Getting up, she gently touched his shoulder, walking past him towards the kitchen. Jay looked on at his mum as she walked away and put his head in his hands, gently rubbing his eyes frustrated.

Jay's meeting with mother dearest had not gone so well. He had tried to convince Elena to look beyond Leya's past which proved futile. Did others not see what he saw in the amazing girl who shared a home with him? She was fun, witty, gorgeous, resilient and personable, not looking the least like what she had been through. He had gotten to understand her choices was as a result of her painful past, but *then again, no one knew her story*, he thought as he gathered his files, placing them into his man bag, leaving the office for the day.

Leya had been sorrowful following the days after her encounter with Jay's mum, but trust Bunmi to cheer her up. "My dear, na ashawo work you do, you no kill person. Abeg leave matter for mattais jare," Bunmi had told her. It wasn't going to be easy to "leave matter" according to Bunmi, but she had resolved to just get on with it. She was a call girl! Her past could not be changed but she was going to accept it with her head held high and move on. It didn't help matters that Jay was getting a lot of stick from friends and family but he was still the same loving man she met. How was a man with so much to lose always willing to defend her? She often wondered. Having a light bulb moment, she decided to do something romantic for Jay – an expression of her feelings for him. Leya had researched during the day when she was alone on romantic ideas, unbeknown to Jay. She had finally gotten everything she needed and was satisfied. Well, except for almost getting into a fight with the seller of the rose petals who thought she was a high society girl and wanted to swindle her. She smiled at her handiwork – the relaxed, soothing ambience with rose petals scattered all over the floor. The lights were dim, lit scented candles placed in strategic positions along with 2 glasses and a bottle of bubbly by the side of the bath. She looked up at the contemporary clock on the wall in the large bathroom suite and undressed, Jay would be home any minute.

He could not wait to hold Leya in his arms as he drove home, listening to the radio. He felt relaxed even after a long day, when she was with him. Jay smiled at the thought of her. The car pulled up in the driveway with Idris running to salute his boss. "Idris, how you dey?" Jay asked, as he stepped out clicking on the remote to lock the car door. "Oga, everything cool sir" Idris responded with a wide grin. "Good" Jay responded. "Make I return go base" Idris said, turning to look towards the gate. Jay smiled, nodding his head in approval. He watched Idris walk back to the gate house and turned towards the front door. His initial reaction at the red petals on the living room floor was confusion, as he followed the trail of the petals to the bathroom. He burst into laughter seeing Leya in the bubble bath, a glass of wine in her hand and a grin on her face. Still giggling he asked,

116

"Productive day studying, yes?" Leya nodded coyly. "Where did you get all of these from?" He asked, looking around impressed at her effort. "My friend Google" Leya replied, Jay chuckled! "So, are you going to join me or just stand there watching" she asked. "Oh, you bet I am," Jay said, hurriedly taking of his shoes almost tripping. He ripped his tie and struggled to balance his foot as he tried to take off his trousers. "Ah ah! Calm down now" Leya laughed. Moments later, they lay together in the bath quietly, listening to the soft music playing, with Jay's arms wrapped around her body from behind and idly running the bubbles over her arms. Leya closed her eyes, her head resting on his chest. "What're you thinking about?" He asked. Eyes still closed, she replied, "That if this is a dream...." her eyes now opened and turning to face him, her supple breast pressed against his chest muscles, ".....I don't want this to ever end." She looked at his lips, running her finger over them, he kissed her finger gently. She turned back to her original position, back facing him. He wrapped his arms around her again and kissed her shoulder. "Do you ever think of finding your birth mom" he asked. She inhaled deeply, "I've had a few thoughts but....." she turned around towards him once again tracing her fingers on his chest, drawing imaginary lines, she continued ".....sometimes I wonder, what if she died many years ago. What if she remarried and wants nothing to do with me. I mean...." she said, looking at him "What if she totally forgot I even existed?" Jay looked at her, his intense gaze once again deeply penetrating her soul. "What?" She asked, "...the way you look at me sometimes scare me" she smiled embarrassingly. Oh, but she loved the way he looked at her! Still looking at her intensely, he said to her, "Have dinner with my business partners and I." "No! No! Noooo" she exclaimed, turning back to her original position quickly. "...and another No!" He let out a little laugh, "That's a lot of No's" he chuckled. "Just to let you I mean it! I'm not going" she said closing her eyes and resting her head on his chest. "C'mon, they'll be there with their partners so it's not like you're going to be there 3 against 1." "Nope" she responded. "I don't want any wahala. Besides, you rich people would gather and order things I've never heard of before. I'll be there trying so hard to fit in" she said. He playfully shook her shoulders, "Pleasseeeeee" he said. "Leave me" she giggled. She turned around to face him, wrapping her arms around his neck. "Your scar, what happened to you" Leya asked. He touched the scar under his eye and giggled, "This! I got into a fight at a club back in University. I wanted to be super hero for this English girl I was dating who got some nasty remarks from these guys at the club. Safe to say, I got some brownie points for that but not without ending up in hospital for stitches and my parents having a panic attack" he laughed. She looked at him with warmth in her eyes, "Any girl would be so lucky to have you. I know I am." "So, does this mean you're coming to dinner with me?" he asked. "Are you sure about this? Knowing who I was? I don't want to...."" Nothing's going to happen" he interrupted, looking at her lips for a few seconds, before grazing his over hers, gently biting her lower lip in a tease. They locked their lips together in a passionate kiss, their hands caressing each other sensually. Leya stopped suddenly and blurted out, "As I gave this your cleaner time off, who will now clean all these nonsense?" she asked looking at the rose petals scattered all over. Jay laughed so hard, his shoulders shook! Cupping her face in his hands and still smiling, he gazed at her for a brief moment – what a girl! As he proceeded to kiss her fervently.

"Love doesn't need to be perfect, it just needs to be true" – *Anonymous*

IO

"Never forget what you are. The rest of the world will not. Wear it like armour, and it can never be used to hurt you"
– Tyrion Lannister (GOT)

Jay was seated with Leya at the plush restaurant, his hand holding hers on his lap. She had agreed to go and looked like a walking goddess in her silver metallic, off shoulder wrap midi dress with pleated blouson sleeves. Her hair was in a bang with a casual fishtail braid hanging on one side of her shoulder. Jay had donned on a classy oxblood coloured wool blazer with black elbow patches over a slim fit high neck black shirt and trousers. Together, they looked like they had walked straight out of a

Vogue magazine turning heads as they walked into the restaurant.

The two business investors and their partners had looked at Jay and Leya admiringly as they approached the table, never short of compliments. The conversation was going well interspersed with laughter and some business talk. "The expansion is going to be great for the state. We are not only building a major factory which will bring us good revenue but creating jobs for the masses" the 1st business man said excitedly. 2nd business man cut in "....the government obviously knows this. Why do you think they jumped at approving the proposal? We are investing millions of naira, doing the hard work and the governor takes the glory." "He has an election coming soon doesn't he?" The 1st business partner chipped in again. "Imagine if we back out now..." Jay said as he poured Leya a drink, "...poor man would have a fit. Greedy bastard." The men laughed! "Let's not bore our ladies" The 1st business man apologised, "So...." he began, when a voice called out, "Leya?" A tipsy man with a friend spotted her as they walked to their table. "How are you? Good to see you again. Still looking as beautiful as ever" he winked at her. Leya almost cowered in embarrassment. "Sorry, my manners" he apologised to the others at the table and tripping over as he stretched his hand to no one in particular, for a handshake. "Jason Daniels?" He asked, almost trying to confirm what he already knew. "Yes" Jay confirmed. He stumbled as he shook Jay's hand looking at Leya and then said out loud. "G house girls be advancing, rolling with the big boys and all." There was an uncomfortable silence at the table, the two ladies looked at each other and then at Leya, a judgmental look written all over their faces. In the most refreshing case of being saved by the bell, another man approached the table apologising, "My friend has had too much to drink tonight, sorry about the unnecessary disruption." As he was being led away, the tipsy guy shouted out, "You changed your mind about sucking dick yet? Need a good suck baby" An awkward silence surrounded the table. The 1st business man cleared his throat uncomfortably, "Alcohol! Makes you do the darndest things."

The drive back home was in total silence. Leya turned to look at Jay, his focus straight ahead. In a hushed tone, she said, "I'm sorry." "It's fine" Jay replied, turning to look at her before taking his eyes back on the road. Leya turned her face towards her side of the window as they continued to drive in silence. The only sound in the car coming from the midnight drive show playing on the radio. What had started as an amazing night, turned out to be one of the most embarrassing moments of her life. She knew who she was and had accepted situations like these might happen. However, what she didn't envisage was how humiliating and awkward it would be. Trust Jay to carry on like this was no big deal but she knew deep inside, he had been mortified, Leya thought! She wished she could protect him, he didn't deserve this!

"You will face many defeats in life, but never let yourself be defeated" – Maya Angelou

Leya and Bunmi were in the kitchen cooking. Bunmi cut the veggies, listening and chuckling at Leya. "I almost died Bunmi. It was like the ground should just open" Leya said, stirring the contents in the pan on fire. "Hah, but I thought our customers are only based on the mainland now. Wetin carry that one go posh restaurant" Bunmi asked. "Hmmm! and Jay was with his business partners and their wives abi girlfriends I don't even know. That's not even my business sef. My own is, if you see the way the idiot now shouted, still don't give head baby ehnnn" Bunmi burst out laughing. "It's not funny o" Leya said. "Sorry now" Bunmi replied, trying so hard not to laugh and continued, "...how was Jay after?" She asked, popping a carrot in her mouth. Leya sighed! "Obviously he was embarrassed, I told him I was sorry. I hated to see him that way." Bunmi looked at Leya, a sudden realisation hit her, "You have fallen in love with him! Leya! This was not the plan o. The plan was to secure the bag and move on." Leya was quiet for a while and then said to Bunmi, "I have never felt this way about a man, ever." Bunmi saw the truth in Leya's eyes and continued, "Anyway sha, sometimes, the best love is the most uncommon. I am rooting for....." Jay walked in, interrupting their conversation. "Hey ladies! Ummm, something smells good" he mentioned, walking over to Leya and kissing her oblivious to the fact Bunmi was right there. She smiled at the two of them as she looked away embarrassed. "Had a good day?" Leya asked, "Um huh" he responded, his gaze fixed on her bare arm, running his fingers up and down them. He turned around to Bunmi, "Bunmi of life! How far now?" "Ah, we can't complain." she responded. He turned back to Leya, "Bunmi joining us for dinner?" Leya nodded. "I'm just going to freshen up and will be back downstairs to join you ladies. "Okay" Leya smiled watching him, undiluted passion in her eyes as he headed out the kitchen. "I go love ooooooo" Bunmi shouted, gesturing with her hands.

Following their Thursday ritual, the boys – Jay, Fred and Tayo had finished their gym session and decided to hang out for a bit. The Lounge was their favourite chill out spot with guys lighting up their cigars, waiters running and up down taking orders. Then, there were the foreign tourists trying to make out the menu and of course, the "runs" girls who came round clearly to look for clients, sitting provocatively and occasionally winking at the guys who made eye contact with them. They had just ordered for drinks when a guy approached their table. "Hey man, you don't remember me right?" He asked. Jay looked at him for a brief moment and recognised him, the douche bag who messed up a great evening with his business partners. "The drunk guy from the other night?" Jay asked. "I'm so, so sorry about that night mehnnn. The name's Lanre," the guy said embarrassingly. Fred and Tayo looked on. "You should be! That was uncalled for" Jay responded sternly, resisting the urge to punch him. Then again, he knew what field day the blogs would have, carrying the news of him hitting someone. If there was one thing he hated, it was being in the papers! "I was an absolute idiot. Too much to drink" he continued. "Just curious though, Leya your woman or just a friend?" The man asked. Tayo and Fred looked at each other, "Any reason why?" Fred interrupted. Lanre continued, "Ahhh my guy, no reason at all. It was just a thought. Beautiful girl! Shame she has to sell her body. I mean, it's not my business but dude, you're big, like you're BIG" stressing on the word big. "A girl like Leya around you? Not a good look." "There you go" Fred muttered to himself. "Nice meeting you again, once again sorry about the other night" Lanre apologised to Jay who nodded nonchalantly. He proceeded to shake Fred and Tayo's hands and walked away. Fred took a sip of his drink, all three of them quiet. "Not a word guys, thank you" Jay cautioned. "Who said we were going to say anything?" Tayo asked chuckling, tipping his cigar into the ash tray. "This is not even about some middle class, upper class bullshit. Babe is a call girl, ashawo" Tayo continued. "Was" Jay interrupted, "...was a call girl. Besides you said you were not going to say a word, with that your wide mouth." They laughed as Jay eventually excused himself to the gents. "This is some messed up shit" Fred said, looking at Jay walking away. "Say that again" Tayo agreed!

Jay approached the gents about to open the door, when he overheard the conversation, "…..as in correct guy from a correct home o. Very respectable family too. Guy wants to cause major scandal because of pussy." Next voice giggled, "Pussy wey don gather very high mileage sef" the voices laughed! "How would a guy like that even think of going out with a babe like Leya?" He heard the first voice say. "…and this na babe wey dey stand for road side o. Who would respect an heir to a conglomerate like the Point holdings knowing his woman na real ashana." The second voice cut in, "Leya! Leya wey me sef don fuck. Girl can wine waist ehnnn. She would not kiss you o, or agree to give you head but dayummm, chick can make you come quickkk." First voice laughed, "at least we have one thing in common with big boy Daniels," "What?" Second voice asked. "We have all entered the same hole now, so dude cannot come and be forming do you know who I am with us" First guy continued, their sarcastic laugh began to make Jay's blood boil. "At least we fit say, ah, that Jay Daniels' babe? Forget! We sef don knack am before!" Jay walked away…….

"Your hardest battle is between what you know in your head and what you feel in your heart"- Anonymous

Jay drove home feeling more confused than ever! The words from the men in the gents kept replaying in his head like a catchy tune. He had feelings for Leya, a deep longing for her. A part of him wanted her so badly and a part knew the endless drama, negativity and bad press their relationship would bring. He was battling conflicting emotions, rushing though his mind like water from a broken tap. He walked through the door to find Leya studying at the table. She looked up as he entered and ran to him in a quick embrace, "Thank you" she said smiling. "What for?" Jay asked, his face tense and expressionless. "For turning my life around. I can't believe I am actually studying for an entrance exam. How cool is that?" she twirled in excitement, Jay forced a smile. "Everything okay?" Leya stopped to ask, noticing his demeanour. He did not show his normal enthusiasm at her silliness. "Yeah, yeah. Just a long day out with the boys" he answered. "I need a shower. Keep studying" he said, kissing her forehead and picking up his keys. Leya looked on as he walked up the stairs, something was amiss. Jay would on a normal night, sit with her and they'll have a recap of the day's events. She sat down to continue studying! Struggling to concentrate, she walked upstairs to find Jay in the shower, his back to the door.

128

Oh, he was sinfully gorgeous! Leya watched as the water dripped down his firm athletic body. She had heard that giving a man a good blow job relieved his stress, but she had never done this before. What if her teeth embarrassed her and bit him? That will be even more stress, she thought. She had to trust herself on this one – after all she had watched a few tutorials. Jay's back still facing her, she stripped naked opening the shower door, he turned. "Thought you were studying" he said, wiping the water from his face. Leya did not say a word as she went down on her knees and took him in her mouth. Jay gasped, closing his eyes as she sucked on him gently, her full lips focusing on the crown, pulling up and down his shaft. Her warm wet tongue caressed and tickled as she continued. He placed his right hand against the bathroom wall for support as he felt his knees trembling, letting go as the tingling sensation rushed through his body. Later they lay in bed spooning, Jay's arms around Leya. He loved to cuddle her that way, it made him feel like her protector! His eyes were closed but not asleep, he still could not believe she had just given him head. He felt special! The first man she had willingly submitted herself to in pleasure - that emotional connection, she called it. He smiled to himself! Leya lay in his arms silent, her eyes were opened but deep in thought. She had just given him head! Well, she hoped she did a good job. Then again, his moan and deep pleasure groans must have meant she aced it. She smiled and whispered, "I love you Jay" closing her eyes to sleep. Jay opened his eyes!

****

He had arrived late to the office. It was a beautiful morning, the glittering sun rays spreading various hues across the bedroom. He had taken one look at Leya sleeping beside him and decided he was going to make her breakfast! He was not the best in the kitchen but he had learnt to make a good English during his university days. They had enjoyed breakfast together in bed amidst laughs and jokes about her first blow job experience. He had to summon the strength to leave her for work, she was a delight to be with! Still day dreaming by his office window with the most amazing view of the city, Fred walked in. "Hey buddy" Jay said as he walked over to give his friend and cousin a manly hug. "Dude" Fred responded. "How's it going?" He asked. "You ask" Jay replied. "Meetings, meetings and then more meetings." Fred laughed, "That's because you're the boss. Well, I passed by

Aunty E's today." Jay smiled, "How's that momma of mine?" He asked. "She's fine, not happy but fine." "Bud" Jay cut in, exasperated. "Hey, don't get me wrong" Fred said. "We've been what? Best friends since we were toddlers and we're also family. Whatever decision you take, I'm still going to be here for you" Fred said. "That means a lot" Jay replied. "However," Fred continued, Jay interrupted raising his hands, "Here we go again!" Fred let out a short laugh. "Got something to show you" as he pulled out a newspaper from his case, placing it on the desk and pushing it over to Jay. "Now this is why Aunty E is unhappy." Jay read the paper in a frown. If there was anything he detested, it was being in the news. "Like dude, for the first time in 40 odd years, we're in the papers for all the wrong reasons. One, you hate being in the papers, two, they are using this story to mask what the Point Holdings company is all about. All we have done for the communities and the country. Three, Uncle Muyiwa would be turning in his grave. You know he was not about this life Jay, we don't need this. And who the heck even wrote this story? Absolutely ridiculous!" Fred said infuriated.

****

Indeed bad news travelled faster than lightning. The press and blogs were having a field day with news of Jay and Leya. His meetings were constantly interrupted with calls and text messages. To make matters worse, Elena would not pick his calls. He had never fallen out with his mother, ever! This was all too much for him and he was beginning to think this was all an illusion and things were never going to be any different. Leya's past would always haunt her and it irked him all the more, that he could not protect her from it. He had decided to let go, somehow, some way. Their evening dinner together was painful to say the least. There was an uncomfortable silence that bothered Leya. Jay had been a bit standoffish with her since he got back, with aloof responses to her questions. She never read blogs or the papers and was unaware of the brouhaha going on. All she cared about was getting back into school, being the best version of herself and making Jay proud. "I have my exam date now" Leya broke the silence, trying to start a conversation. "Good" Jay said matter of factly. Silence again! "Have I upset you?" Leya asked worryingly. "No", Jay said standing up, "I have some files I need to go through for a meeting tomorrow. I'll be upstairs in a bit."

He walked away from the dining area as Leya looked at him distraught.

She tossed and turned in bed all night. Something was not right! Had his friends and family convinced him about her? She thought. As the first ray of sunlight hit the room, she took a shower and went downstairs to the kitchen. Breakfast like a king might do wonders, she thought. After all, Jay loved her cooking. He came downstairs already dressed up for work which was unusual, as most mornings, she had to fight him off her so he could get ready for the day. "You didn't sleep in the bedroom last night" Leya said to him concerned. "I'm sorry, I fell asleep doing work. Did you have a good night?" He asked. "Couldn't sleep much" she responded. "Why" Jay asked, opening the fridge and pouring himself some juice. "I don't know, I feel like I have offended you in some way. I just need to know if I've upset you?" her eyes welled up. He looked at her, it broke his heart whenever he saw her distressed, "Look at me," he said, holding both her arms. "It's not you okay, it's me" he said. "Now, I need to run" putting the juice down and kissing her forehead. "I made you breakfast." He looked over the kitchen counter and saw the breakfast. "I really don't think you should be doing all of this."

"But I love doing them, especially for you" she replied, moving towards him. As she tried to hug him, he pulled away slightly, "No, I think we should give all this cooking a break. That is why I pay for the services of a chef." An uncomfortable atmosphere filled the kitchen, "I'll see you later" he said, walking away, leaving Leya astounded.

****

The next few days felt so lonely! It had become a daily routine for Jay to leave the house very early and come back home late. He avoided her like a deadly plague. Bunmi had mentioned he was probably under pressure and Leya needed to bring her A game into the bedroom. She lay on the bed in a transparent white lingerie waiting for Jay. However, her plan had fallen through when he walked into the bedroom, kissed her cheeks and went back downstairs. He had failed to notice her lingerie or just pretended not to have noticed. Oh, but he did! He wanted to hold her in his arms and make slow sweet passionate love to her but a chaotic mix of emotions burned so badly within him, he had to summon the courage to walk away and not lead her on any further.

Jay had spent most of the hours at work each day not because he didn't love Leya, but because he hated himself for what he was doing to her. He could see the pain in her eyes whenever he walked through the door. A part of him wanted her so badly and a part of him knew it was for the best if he pushed her away subtly. Standing by the window in his office, he picked up his phone to dial her number. Hesitating for a second, he looked at the phone and put it back in his pocket. Jay had felt like a coward when Leya tried to call him, waiting for him at home for hours and he did not show up. He had responded by text saying he was with Fred and it was too late to drive back home so he was going to stay the night. His stomach churned at his own lies, for the truth was, he had agreed to have dinner with a very apologetic Amara and spent the night at hers. The date night had turned into a mini argument when Jay would not touch her once they got to her apartment! How could he? He was hopelessly in love with a woman whose heart he was systematically breaking. It was dawn when Jay left Amara's apartment, his energy zapped from her constant yelling and screaming. He had gone over to Fred's for a change of clothes and headed on to the office. Priscilla, his personal assistant knocked on his door, "Come in" Jay said.

"Sorry sir, there's a lady here to see you" she said, standing by the door. "Lady? What lady and what does she want?" He asked. "Not sure" Priscilla responded. "Not sure?" Jay asked. "I did not employ you not to be sure of what someone here to see me wants. That's like saying....." "It was my fault" a voice interrupted. Jay and his secretary turned towards the door. It was Leya, looking as beautiful as ever. She had donned on a black tailored blazer dress with detailed pleats trim and a pair of leopard print suede Louboutin heels, her hair held up in a ponytail with loose curls hanging on each side of her face. "This, this is the lady sir" Priscilla stuttered. "I thought you might not want to see me so I told a little lie to your PA" she said entering as Priscilla hurriedly walked out. "What're you doing here?" Jay asked surprised, walking over and closing the door behind them. "I just came to ask you a question?" She said. "Okay" Jay replied, taking a seat and looking at her. "You look very beautiful by the way" he smiled. "You have been avoiding me lately" she started, ignoring his compliment. "I ermmm, I, I can leave your house if I have overstayed my welcome. I feel I have caused you too many problems and you cannot tell me because this is just who you are. The best man I've ever met." Jay got up and tried to say something. She gestured with her hands, "No, please, let me finish." Jay sat partially on his desk watching Leya pace up and down as she continued to speak. "Before I met you, I, I did not know what being valued felt like, I was just this girl, selling her body for coins just to survive. I was a girl, with no family, no one to run to if I had any problems. For goodness sake, I did not even know what an orgasm felt like" letting out a short laugh as the tears began to flow from her eyes. Jay got up to go to her but she gestured a no with her hands as she continued pacing, "....then I met you. You made me feel so special, got me to go back to school. Even stood for me when your family knew what scandal this was going to bring. I am only here to say thank you. Thank you for your beautiful affection, for the wonderful times we have spent together. I feel the dream has come to an end." "No! No, this dream is not over" Jay rushed over to her, wiping her tears with his hands and kissing all over her face. "I'm sorry sweet pea, I'm so sorry for making you feel this way. I've been under so much pressure lately from all sides and it just got overwhelming. I'm sorry, I really am," cupping her face and gazing into her eyes. "I am still attracted to the lady I met that night many moons ago, fighting with Bayo and then cursing the guy she was meant to meet up with" he teased her smiling. "I want you now just as much as I wanted you then. Damn it! This is not over." He exclaimed, kissing her with such intensity, fuelled by passion as his hand frantically cleared the papers on his desk, laying Leya gently on it.

II

"Crying is a way your heart speaks, when your mouth can't explain how broken your heart is" - Anonymous

The sun was blazing hot and humid! The rush cool of air from a moving vehicle was as soothing as a quick plunge into a pool. Some pedestrians chose to ease their discomfort drinking some form of ice cold drink whilst others held hand fans.

Leya had been to visit Bunmi who had complained of being unwell. The feeling of being back at G house was surreal. She had left that life behind, all thanks to a chance encounter with a man she had fallen so in love with. Like a flower, she had blossomed along with a sense of purpose for the first time in her life. "Mehnnnn Leya, I'm worried about you o. This one all his family members are putting pressure on him like this." Bunmi continued, "I do not doubt the love he has for you rara. I have witnessed it myself but pressure ehnn, pressure can make somebody just change." "I love him Bunmi. I love him with every fibre of my body and soul" Leya said to her. "O' ti tan" Bunmi exclaimed in the local dialect, raising her hands in defeat. "It is finished. Soul has entered inside the love" she teased. "Bunmi now, I'm serious. Besides I came here to stay with you for the night because you said you're not feeling well" Leya said, giving Bunmi a suspicious look. Just as Bunmi was about to respond puppy faced, Leya's phone rang. She screamed in excitement whilst listening, startling Bunmi. "Thank you sir, thank you" she said, jumping up and down. When the caller hung up, Bunmi asked curiously, "What was that about?" "Bunmiiiiiiii" Leya shouted, shaking her. "What is it? Stop shaking me like that. You want to give me epilemsip?" Leya laughed, "Epilepsy Bunmi, Epilepsy." "Ehnn you sha know what I mean," Bunmi responded. "I got accepted into the state college for my Diploma. I passed the entrance exams." Bunmi started to dance and sing elated, "We have a very big God o, he is always by our side, a very big God o, by our side, by our side." She suddenly stopped singing, her hands on her waist, "Wait o! We must pop champagne." "Pop what?" Leya asked giggling, picking up her bag. "Ah, ah, where are you going?" "I, am, goiinnng, tooooo, pop champagne with my maann" she said stressing on her words. Bunmi called out as Leya walked towards the door, "but I'm still not feeling well now. Na wa o, I go love" before she went back to singing and dancing just as Leya shut her door.

Leya could not believe what was happening to her. The universe was aligned to her desires and lines were falling on to her in pleasant places. She smiled at the thought of Jay finding out her hard work had paid off. Nights of endless study and research had generated success and she was excited about this whole new lease of life! She stopped by the wine shop, buying a bottle of champagne and excitedly, talked to herself, "New life. New beginnings" as she boarded her Uber to Jay's house. Arriving at the mansion, she knocked on the gate as Idris opened surprised to see her! "Ah Aunty Leya, I been think say na tomorrow you dey come o" he said apprehensively. She laughed! "I wan surprise your Oga." Idris had an unease about him but Leya paid no notice as she made the long stretch of walk towards the house, swinging her bottle exhilarated. Her excitement doubled when she realised Jay was home, the velar he driven out with in the morning, parked in its bay. She opened the door but it appeared locked from the inside. This was a moment of surprise and she didn't want to ruin it by knocking on the door. Taking out her key, she tried to unlock the door to no avail. Sighing, she rang the doorbell, no answer. She rang the doorbell repeatedly until Jay finally opened the door. Eyes wide open and petrified as one who had just seen a ghost, he exclaimed, "Leya! You're home. I thought you were staying the night with Bunmi?" "Yes, I knowww" Leya smiled, "but I've got some good news to share" brushing past Jay into the living room. Idris watched from a distance, an anxious look on his face as Jay closed the door. Leya rushed to him, wrapping her arms around him. Oh, how he made her feel! She had never felt a love as deep as this and she loved this man. Trailing her fingers over his bare chest, she said flirtatiously "…and besides, I missed you, I missed kissing you, I missed being in your arms, I……" suddenly a voice interrupted. "Jay, what's keeping you?" Leya looked up and Amara walked down the stairs wearing nothing but a bath robe, revealing her smooth thighs up to her crotch area. She had intentionally pushed the robe off her shoulders to reveal the mound of her breast. "W-w-what's going on here" Leya muttered, her face paralysed with fear. Jay rubbed his face in frustration! *This was not the plan*, he thought to himself. Amara had played on his emotion, asking to come over for a final talk, they had reminisced about the good times and what had gone wrong. He enjoyed her company when she wasn't playing games, but unfortunately, he had outgrown her sneaky ways. The night was intended to heal, according to Amara. She was then going to be on her way and he could focus on getting his family convinced about the love of his life – Leya! "Jay!" Leya interrupted his thoughts, moving towards him. "Jay! Are we going to entertain this hoe tonight?" Amara shouted irritated. "She's had her fun, we discussed this, what is she doing here? Oh, you thought you had your claws in my man ah? Because you're a harlot skilled in bedmatics?" Leya's eyes began to fill up. "You come here from nowhere, trying to take....." "Shut up Amara!" Jay shouted. "Jay!" Amara yelled surprised, "You're going to stick up for this hoe?" "Just shut up and go back upstairs" Jay shouted again. "I'm not going anywhere! I'm going to stand here and wat...." Jay held Amara's arm, pulling her to a corner in the living area, "One more word Amara, one more word and you're out my door." She struggled from his hold aggressively and stomped upstairs angrily.

Jay turned to Leya, "You told me it wasn't over just to ridicule me?" Leya asked white faced covered in tears. Jay moved over to hold her, she stepped back. "No! Don't come near me!" There was something in that shout, a raw pain behind it. "Leya, listen to me" Jay tried to move closer to her again. She moved back, "You're like all of them. All of them! All you people do is take from me, hurt me and break me. All you people do is take from me, hurt me and break me" she repeated, falling to the ground and wrapping her arms around her body. Jay watched, he knew! Her action was nothing but a shield from pain. She was protecting herself like a little child in a corner, hiding from the big monster. The bottle of bubbly still in her right hand, Jay looked on helplessly. He went over to hold her but she got up, boldly wiping her face, "I'm a strong girl, you could have told me you couldn't do this anymore. I, I would, I.....I love you" she whispered. "You showed me what true love was. The first man I ever kissed, the first man I willingly gave myself to. The first man I gave my heart to." She let out a psychotic laugh and then broke down in tears. Amidst heavy tears, she continued to speak as Jay watched. Every look of anguish in her eyes tore his heart to pieces but she would not let him move close to her. "You should have just let me be on my way that night at your hotel. Why did you ask me to come here? Why?" She asked. "I asked you to come here because I love you. I fell in love with you the moment you got that call in the elevator" Jay said almost on the verge of tears himself. "Love. No one has ever loved me? It's all pretence to take from me. You all use me and leave me" she said to herself. Looking at the bottle in her hand and letting out a chuckle, she looked at him, "I came to celebrate my acceptance into business school. I passed Jay," her make up streamed with lines of tears on her face, her voice broken. "I don't think this is of any use now. You need it more than I do, seeing as you are back with madam." She walked over to hand the bottle to him and tripped, sending the bottle high up in the air and crashing hard on the marbled floor. Instinctively, he rushed over to her but she got on her knees, picking up the shards of glass with her bare hands, each swoop cutting deep into her flesh as blood flowed over her hands and fingers. She didn't care about the pain, it was a sort of soothing comfort for her. "Stop it! Leya! Please, stop this." Jay panicked, taking her blood covered hand away from the broken glass scattered all over the floor. "No! No, I have to clean your floor. It's my fault, I let this happen. I need to clean it, it's my fault" she let go of his grip, frantically sweeping the floor with her bruised hand, her flesh exposed. Jay ran into the kitchen. Anxiously, he opened the cupboards trying to find his first aid box. Heaving a sigh of relief as the box stuck out in the corner of the cupboard, he ran out to see Leya standing, blood dripping to the floor from her wounded hand. For the first time, he saw a vulnerability, a hurt and a spirit so broken. Jay held her hand, she let go. "You are so bound by your rules that you cannot smell the rose even with all her thorns." In a state of despair, Jay tried to say something but she interrupted, whispering in defeat, "Why is it no one wants me? Why do they always hurt me?" She headed towards the door, her blood marking the floor with every step she took. Jay ran to hold her back, missing his step, his foot landed on one of the shards. He screamed in pain as the large shard stuck under his foot, watching helplessly as Leya opened the door with her bloodied hands and walked out.

It had begun to rain, heavily! Leya walked by the road, oblivious to the beeping cars or the people scampering about, trying to take cover from the torrential rain. The drops of water drenched her hair and her body, washing away her blood as she walked. Arriving at G house, Leya knocked faintly on Bunmi's door. Taking one look at Leya as she opened the door, Bunmi quickly grabbed Leya into her arms, holding her as she broke down in tears. Kneeling and holding each other, Bunmi tried to soothe her baby girl as they soaked in the pouring rain.

12

"An unforseen situation...An unexpected turn of events. In the face of those, you too will find your true self" – Shougo Makishima

Jay arrived G house a week later. Not realising how deep the shard cut through his foot, he had been put on bed rest after his stitches. Neither Leya nor Bunmi were picking his calls and he was worried sick. Events of that night kept replaying in his head, a crazy mix of emotions flowed through him each time he remembered. He had not meant to hurt her and seeing her spirit crushed at the sight of Amara was all he could take. He wanted to speak to her, check she was okay, assure her that this feeling he had towards her was real. At this point he could care less who

148

was for or against what they felt for each other. She had come into his life as sudden as a bolt of thunder and her energy radiated in different hues that lit up a room when she was present.

He parked his car by the open gutters of Gbese house stepping out when Don dadaa walked over to him, "Boss man, I vex for you o, I vex well well." Jay looked at him confused, "Wetin happen my guy" He asked. "Ah bros, if you wan bad person for G house, no be Leya na. That girl na better person o. Forget say she be Ashiii. She be correct person I dey tell you" Don dadaa replied, gyrating and gesturing at Jay like a rap artist shooting a music video. "If no be say you be my guy ehnnn, I for arrange with boys make them kpeme you" Don stated. "The reason I am here. I need to talk to her" Jay said. "You fit protect my machine?" he asked, pulling out a bundle of cash for Don. "Haaaahhh, this one plenty o. Boss boss! Oga di Oga. No wahala, no shaking. Na my life I go take protect this machine." Don looked at the money handed to him, grinning from ear to ear. "Thank you" Jay said as he walked towards the wooden gate of G house with Don dadaaa propped on Jay's car protectively. From a distance, two ghetto chics with short nappy hair dyed in a bright blue and the other a purple colour approached Don. The blue haired girl wore a bandeau crop top revealing her belly rolls, pierced belly button, tattooed arm and a mini skirt exposing her cellulite thighs. She walked close to him smiling flirtatiously, "Don dadaa." Her long claw like acrylic nails caressing his bare chest. "Wetin happen" he asked unfazed by her actions. "Don noww" the one in the bright purple hair, wearing a ripped denim hot pant and a slim line vest top shouted loudly, "Let us take picture with this car now" they tried to coerce him flirtatiously. "See ehnn, if you like, rub my hair, rub my chest, e no work. No picture." "Haba, Don baba, just one picture for Instagram" she continued. "Please nowww" they pleaded in unison. Don sized them up frowning, "E go cost una o." "How much" they asked. "2k each" Don responded, his gaze straight ahead. "Hah, on top person car, mtcheww" Blue haired girl hissed angrily. "Oya no picture, make una carry unaself dey go." Don gestured for them to leave. "Ehnn, we sef dey go. 2k on top person motor" purple haired girl put her arm around her friend's shoulder as they walked away cussing him under their breath. "See them, awon local slay queens. Wan take picture with this machine. Bicycle sef, una papa no get" as Don propped himself on Jay's car like he owned it, taking a selfie with a wide grin.

Jay walked into G house just as Bunmi was heading out. She saw Jay, blatantly ignoring him, she kissed her lips in annoyance, walking past and shoving him aside. He calmly pulled her back, "Woh"*meaning 'Look! in the local Yoruba dialect*. "I'm not Leya o. In fact I'm a nice person not to just gather these hungry area boys, make them beat you wella" she said angrily. "I know you're angry with me, I deserve that but Bunmi, I need your help, please. I need to speak to Leya. She's not picking my...." "Leya is not here!" Bunmi interrupted. "What do you mean she's not here?" He asked. "Exactly what I mean" Bunmi retorted. "Where is she? Please Bunmi, I just want to speak to her, explain, please" Jay pleaded. Bunmi looked at him and felt the genuineness in his voice. She composed herself better and calmly responded, "The night she came here, you left her broken to the core. I have never seen her that way, ever! I had to give her sleeping tablet because she would not sleep." "I wanted to come over that night but I hurt my foot, could not drive or walk on it." Jay explained. "Her hand" he stated, "Is her hand okay?" He asked. "Well, she would not go and see a doctor so I wrapped it up in bandage" Bunmi replied. Jay rubbed his head in frustration. "Yesterday, I decided to go out and get her something to eat. Something she would like. I returned and she wasn't here, just a piece of paper on the bed. I opened the paper...." Bunmi's voice began to choke as she recounted," I opened the paper and....let me show you." She walked back to her room, bringing a piece of paper to Jay.

Jay opened to read: *"My dearest Bunmi, my sister, my friend, my mother. I knew if I did not leave this way, you will never let me leave but this place has nothing to offer me. Lagos has offered me nothing but pain and constant struggles. Thank you for being there for me, thank you for the nights I cried talking about my birth mom, for the nights I woke you up with my nightmare screams. Thank you for the many laughs, taking over my fights. I could never repay you enough for taking a stranger in and treating her like a sister from day one. You mentioned things were getting serious with Rufai and you have always dreamed of owning your own Buka. My ears always bled from listening to your Buka dreams. Under your pillow, I have left you with money. Make your dream come true! You warned me about falling in love but I was too naive. Ashawo wey no get sense! My darling friend, we may or may never meet again, but one thing is for sure, I hold you in my heart forever. Love always, your baby girl!*

Jay rubbed his eyes, trying to mask his tears. He cleared his throat, "Do you have any idea where she would go?" He asked Bunmi, who also wiped her own tears. "No, she never mentioned anywhere she liked to go. Her dreams died until she met you. She was so happy about going back to school" Bunmi replied. "Ah, I'll miss my friend. My baby girl" Bunmi broke down in tears, walking back to her room and leaving Jay standing there helpless. He felt cold, his body shivered. As he turned to leave, a voice called out to him. He turned to see Charity walking up to him and flirtatiously running her fingers over his arms whilst checking to see that no one, especially Bunmi, was watching. "If you ever need a good time, I mean, a really good time, just let me know." Jay stood there looking at her, his mind preoccupied. "I'll bear that in mind" he replied and walked away, leaving Charity standing at the same spot feeling as though she had accomplished a major feat. She checked her surrounding to make sure no one saw her, before walking back to her room smiling.

Leya had snuck out of G house when the girls were sleeping which was normally mid mornings. The last thing she wanted was for them to see her with a travel bag and ask a million questions she could not answer. Taking one final look at Gbese house, a place she called home for years, she walked towards the main road. Arriving at the bus station, she walked to the ticket box, "Hello, when is the next bus leaving" she asked. The ticket attendant looked at her and smiled at the beauty before him. "In 30 minutes. Sisi where are you going?" Leya was silent for a few minutes, she had not thought this through. Where was she even going? "I don't know" she replied. He looked at her perplexed, "You don't know keh?" She looked around the station and then at him, "Where is the next bus going to?" "Abuja" he answered. "Can I have a single ticket?" With a concerned look washed over his face, he asked, "Are you sure?" "Yes" she replied. He shrugged his shoulders handing her a ticket. Thanking him and collecting her ticket, she boarded the bus finding a window seat. Leya lay her head on the glass frame and closed her eyes.

"So, it's true when all is said and done, grief is the price we pay for love" - E.A. Bucchianeri

The days that passed after Leya left had no meaning to Jay Daniels. Like a ship adrift at sea, his mind was uncontrollable. He missed her terribly, like a badly wounded soldier on a battlefield, he had given up on life. Living a life of recluse, he shut everyone out, fired his chef, unresponsive to Idris' greetings, and missed work and stake holder meetings. He was all over the blogs and Elena was terribly worried about her only child. She knew her son loved Leya, and the disturbing actions of his present state of mind only further buttressed the point. Elena had to do something and fast! Possessing an emotion only a mother could elicit, she had managed to get him out of his house, moving back in with her and soliciting the assistance of the most renowned psychotherapist in the country, all to no avail. Eventually, the psychotherapist had decided to call it a day since Jay would not even acknowledge her presence each time she came over. She had left assuring Elena that his pain was only for a time and a season. He always stayed in his childhood bedroom, door locked. Food was only but a satisfaction he was not interested in. Elena was in anguish! Her only child was slowly slipping into a dark abyss before her eyes and she was helpless. She knocked on his door, no response. She tried to open the door, "Jason Olugbenga

Daniels, open this door. Shi le'kun. Gbenga mi, how long are you going to continue like this okoh mi?" She called to him behind the door. Fred arrived, rushing over to his aunty and quickly kissing her on the cheek. Just like Elena, every action Fred had taken, proved futile to get his cousin out of his current mental state. He was deeply concerned about his best friend and blood. "Has he at least eaten anything?" Fred asked. Elena shook her head in despair, Fred knocked, banging on the door, "Jay! Dude, c'mon now, please open this door. Please." Fred and Elena kept knocking and pleading as Jay lay on the bed, oblivious to the sounds coming from outside, his eyes to the ceiling watching the chandelier swirl.

****

Leya came off the bus after it had parked at the station. She looked around not knowing where to go from there. Fatigue was written all over her with streams of tears that had engraved long faint lines on her face. The journey had been one of sadness, her pain could only be described as a hot knife cutting deep through her flesh and every time she remembered her loss, it was another deep excruciating cut to her already damaged mental state. She walked a few metres, still observing her strange surroundings. Finding a rock to sit on, she looked up at the cloudy skies, where did she go from here? Turning around, she saw a passer-by, "Hello" she called, her voice faint and tired. The young man stopped to look at her. "What is this place called?" He answered. "Are there any guesthouse around here" she asked. He answered once again, directing Leya on where to find available lodge. *She was very beautiful but harboured a pain in her eyes*, he thought. "Thank you." she said to him. "You're new around here?" he asked, She nodded. "Welcome. My name is Aminu." She nodded again – words seemed to fail her. "Anyways, I hope you have a good time here." As he proceeded to be on his way, he turned to her, "...your eyes are very sad. Whatever it is, this too shall pass, Insha Allah." Smiling at her, he walked away. Darkness had begun to fill the horizon and the stars appeared by the time Leya found a place to lodge. It was just a simple room with a bed and a small table. She placed her bag on the floor and sat on the bed in melancholy, the emotions flooding in as she put her face in her hands and cried.

13

"Don't cry when the sun is gone, because the tears won't let you see the stars" – Violeta Parra

Fred, Tayo and Chuks were at the Polo club, laughing and drinking when Jay walked in. He looked really good! It had been a year since the whole Leya saga and it had finally taken the intervention of Uncle T for him to open up and accept what he was going through. Some days were difficult, some days good and he was beginning to look forward to a fresh start for each day ahead. The search for Leya had been unsuccessful, it was almost as if she had disappeared off the face of the earth. He missed her terribly but that always messed with his mind as he then began to wonder what might have happened to her. Was she okay? Was she being exploited once again or attacked. Had she committed suicide which he was never going to forgive himself for? Did she go back to selling her body? Where was Leya! The thoughts always drove him insane. With Uncle T's persistence, he had taken up a new sport – Polo and also travelled for a while, visiting new countries and experiencing their sights and sounds. He felt ready to reconnect with his loved ones. He owed it to them for the love and support they had provided him, *but what about Leya, who was there for her*, he always thought to himself. Wherever she was, he hoped to God she was okay and safe!

The boys turned to him, "Heyyy, look who's back" Fred said excitedly, as he got up to give Jay a hug. The others followed to hug him too, all elated to see him as they sat back down. "How's it going?" Tayo asked. "Yeah, cool." Jay responded, taking a drink from Fred and sipping. "I'm sorry about what happened" Tayo continued, "Dude, you loved that girl man" Fred chipped in. Jay silently sipped his drink. "Well…" he began when Fred interrupted, "I see Amara left the country again?" "Yep" Jay replied matter of factly, "….never to return I hope to God" he frowned, taking another sip of his drink. The boys burst out in laughter. "Glad to see you back to being Jay" Tayo smiled, patting Jay on the back. "Guy, I have a list of eligible spinsters just waiting in line to get that Jay call you know" Chuks teased. "Like dude, these ladies hit me up on Insta and I'm thinking yooooo, I'm hot like fire. Then all they're asking about is Jay Daniels, Jay Daniels" he finished. Fred said to him, "Chuks, this is not good for your reputation. Major low blow! How will a lady enter my DM and be asking about another guy?" Fred giggled. "Is Jason Daniels your friend? Can I have his number? I didn't know you were buddies with Jason, he's so hot" Chuks mimicked a female voice. Jay laughed! "I'll start blocking all of them" he continued, "Fine boy like me and I'll.......Well, dayumm" he exclaimed, looking over the bar. They all turned to follow his gaze. Two ladies had arrived, walking over to sit at the bar. They ordered some drinks engaging in a seemingly interesting conversation as they laughed occasionally. "Oya dude, time to shoot your shot" Fred prodded Chuks. "Let's see if you got it" Tayo teased Chuks. "We'll be watching" Jay notified, trying hard not to laugh at a tensed Chuks. Chuks stood up, straightening his Armani t-shirt and walked over to the ladies as Fred, Tayo and Jay looked on chuckling. He approached their table, said something to them, they smiled as he turned briefly to the guys and winked. He pulled up a seat, engaging in a conversation with the ladies for a few minutes. "I'm sure they're asking him who the guys sitting over here are" Fred chuckled as Tayo laughed, "Chuks, commander in chief of the curved guys association" The boys laughed. After a few minutes, he got up from the ladies table and walked back to the guys mouthing a "Who's the daddy?" as the ladies followed behind. "Guys, may I introduce you to Aisha and Damilola," a wide grin on Chuks face. "Fred, Tayo and Jay" he said pointing at each guy as the ladies shook each hand. Damilola got to Jay, they looked at each other for a few seconds before Damilola said to him smiling, "Pleasure to meet you."

"Date nights, the best nights" – Pookie Sho

Damilola was a tall, attractive, highly educated young lady with a bottom hourglass figure and smaller bust. This reflected in the dark ochre, form fitting deep v neck midi dress with thigh split she had on, which further accentuated her hips. Her long black natural hair was in a side part twist strands that fell on her bosom. Jay had been attracted to her intelligence when they met the first time. Besides, there had been some sort of chemistry when they met at the Lounge that they had agreed to see each other again. As she sat across Jay in one of the city's restaurants, the waiter brought over their drinks and Jay nodded in appreciation to him. "So, Damilola," "Please call me Dami" She replied, her voice warm and sweet. "Ookayy Dami" Jay said smiling, "I never got to ask what you do, the last time we met" Jay said. She smiled at him, "Well, I'm currently the head of operational excellence at Labspace Company Ltd." "Oh wow! Big girl doing big things I see." "Hmm....." she replied, "I hope so." "Labspace ah? We have worked with them in the past. I assume you're taking over from Mr Mensa right?" He asked. "Yes, I am actually. He retired a few months ago and here I was, back from studying at the London School of Economics, looking to make my mark here. Job opening came up, I applied and the rest they say, is history." Jay looked at Dami as she continued to speak but Leya's face was all he saw - her gregarious, non-pretentious personality and the way she made him laugh at her comments. Dami was a total contrast to Leya. She was articulate, very composed with great etiquette. Almost perfect in her dealings which made Jay nervous enough to not utter a wrong word or curse out. With Leya, he could let his guard down but Dami reminded him of his mother – always so poised! As she laughed, he saw Leya sitting across from him laughing her head off, her perfect face as radiant as the sun in all its glory. His thoughts were interrupted with a "Don't you agree?" jolting him back to reality and Dami. "Sorry, what was it you said?" He asked. "I'm offended" Dami pretended to be upset. "Here I am, talking my head off and you were not even listening." "Ahhh Please don't be upset" Jay said to her. "Looking at you got me lost in thought." Dami blushed, playing with the strands of twist laying over her left breast and responded, "I'll take that as a compliment. Cheers to many more dates" as their wine glasses clicked.

Jay had gradually eased back into work, spending more hours trying to make up for the lost times, catching up on projects and documents that required his signature. Fred tapped on the slightly opened office door, sticking his head in, he said "Hey." Jay raised his head, "Hey" standing up and walking over to give Fred a man hug. "What brings you here this morning" Jay asked, going back to sit down. "Dude" Fred sighed rubbing his head as he took a seat. "Cabinet meeting, then to the airport to meet the delegates for the conference. Back for a performance review meeting with the manager, lunch with Marie...." Jay laughed,

"Fully packed day I see. You might want to drink some red bull mate." "It's so hard to be a man sometimes but Marie keeps me sane after a long busy day" Fred replied. "Speaking of Marie, how is she?" Jay asked. "She's alright. Making her own mark in the fashion industry, I'm proud of her. That reminds me" Fred said "....and why I am here this morning actually, before I set off on my day." "What is it?" Jay asked. "Hmmm, a little bird tells me you had a date with a certain lady we all met" Fred said mischievously. Jay chuckled as he signed some documents, "Bloody little bird is no other than Chuks." Fred burst out laughing, "Well?" Fred asked. "Well," Jay replied. "It was good...." "Just good?" Fred asked slightly disappointed. "What else do you want me to say?" Jay raised his head to look at Fred. Fred got up, "For starters, you can say, amazing, awesome, great, bla bla bla," looking at Jay as he sorted through some papers. Silence engulfed the office so much so, one could hear a pin drop as Jay continued to sign his documents. Fred watched his cousin silently and said quietly, "You haven't forgotten her have you?" Jay looked up at Fred.

"A question not asked is a door not opened" – Marilee Adams

164

Bunmi's Buka style food joint had been a huge success. The tables were filled with customers of all age and sizes. The servers were always seen running and up down catering to the needs of their customers. All thanks to Leya, Bunmi no longer ran the streets and had suddenly gained some new found respect amongst the locals as the G house girl who turned her life around. Indeed, things had become even more serious with Rufai, one of her G house returning client who owned a local mechanic workshop in the area. She had moved in with Rufai after he and his family had gone to her village to perform the introduction and traditional marriage ceremony. Bunmi felt content at this stage in her life – she was a Madam!

Amidst the rush, Bunmi shouted out at one of her girls, "Toyin, Tooooyinnnn. Hah! Where is this girl now? Toyinn." Toyin ran up to Bunmi, plates in her hands, "Yes ma." Frowning, Bunmi looked at her up and down. "So, ordinary five plates, five plates, I said go and wash." "Ma, sorry ma. Patience told me to put the plate down and help her to stir the Amala." Toyin said apologetically. "Ehnnn!!! In my own Buka, my own Buka!" Bunmi shouted. "I am giving orders, one mosquito is also giving order as the second in command that she be ehnn? Where is she?

Patience, Patienceee" she called out in high pitch. "Ma" Patience acknowledged in a panicked state, running towards her Madam. "Ehen, Aunty. You get shares for my business?" Patience looked at her confused, "Erm no Ma." "In fact, let me ask you again? When I started this my business, did you give me one naira?" "Hah, no ma," Patience responded raising both hands in the air and then back down stressing on her truth. "Okay o, so why will I tell Toyin, Toyin go and bring me plate for customer. Then you will now tell Toyin, Toyin leave plate, come and turn Amala?" "Hey!" Patience put her hands on her head in trepidation, "Sorry Ma, she did not tell me it was you who sent her." "Ehen, so if it was not me who sent her, this is how you will be acting like second madam in my own business abi? Oya, go and take your final pay, leave my Buka." "Haaaahhhh, madam, please no" Patience said as she knelt down to beg, holding and slightly pulling on Bunmi's African print maxi dress. "You want to tear my fine dress abi? I said go, before you will come and use evil eye to collect my business." "Hah, Madam, I am a sister in Christ o, I cannot do you evil" Patience said, still on her knees. "Sister in Christ kor, Daughter of ……." at that moment Jay stepped into the Buka. Bunmi quickly dispersed Patience and

Toyin. "You people should go, I'll finish with you later." Patience got up walking away, Toyin followed as Patience tried to hit her for snitching. Bunmi's demeanour completely changed, "Hi" she said to Jay slightly embarrassed. "Hello Bunmi" he responded. "Please, sit" directing him to a chair. He sat and looked around shaking his head in approval. "Nice place you got here." "All thanks to my baby girl" Bunmi replied smiling. "How can I help you" she asked. "Well, I ermmm, I, I just wanted to check if you've heard from Leya at all?" Bunmi looked at him in an almost pitiful way. "No, not at all. She left with nothing, not even her phone and baby girl was terrible with keeping numbers so there is no way she would even be able to call me." Bunmi said. "I miss her all the time and I hope she is fine wherever she is. Hah! My Leya." Bunmi continued, Jay was silent!

14

"Turn your wounds into wisdom" – Oprah Winfrey

❝ Yes, bring those ones down. Its old stock anyways, we may have to reduce the prices" Tina, the middle aged fabric shop owner said. Leya climbed the ladder and brought the clothes down. "Thank you my dear" the woman smiled at Leya. She had met Aunty T as she affectionately called her, by a stroke of luck. Going from business to business enquiring about any job openings, Leya had ended up at a bureau de change where Aunty Tina had arrived to purchase some currencies. She had overheard the conversation between the sales girl and Leya, observing her quietly. As Leya turned to leave after yet another rejection, Aunty T had stopped her and offered her a job if she was interested. Leya could not believe it, the offer was sweet melody to her ears! The last thing she wanted to do was walk the streets again and Aunty T with her chubby round face always lit up in a smile, had made that possible.

She loved working for Aunty T who was one of the nicest, personable woman she had ever met. The money wasn't great but at least it paid her rent and the basic necessities she required, including saving up for night school which she had found out about, from her many conversations with Aunty T. Well, the conversations Leya wanted to talk about! Not all days were great and sometimes, she wished she could crawl into a hole and stay there forever. Being strong was the only option she had and was determined to take it one day at a time. Work kept her mind busy but it was the lonely quiet nights that were her demons. She missed Bunmi so much but in her despair, had left her phone back at G house with no back up of any sort. Leya had resolved to start all over again hoping that someday, just maybe, their paths would cross again. Jay was but a memory she blanked, it was never real she told herself. He had been a figment of her imagination and like all the others who had hurt her before, a distant memory. Aunty Tina had once mentioned to her how great a business acumen she had, she was therefore going to turn her lemons into lemonade, and someday, she, Leya, the once queen of the deep dark night, was going to be her own boss!

"T, T" another middle aged woman called out as she entered the shop all smiles. Aunty Tina smiled "Ah, my dear friend" hugging the lady. "Please sit," offering her a chair. "What can I offer you?" Aunty Tina asked. "Just water" the lady responded. "Leya, my dear bring some water for Aunty Reggie. So, to what do I owe this visit" Tina asked. "Nothing o, I cannot visit my friend again? I went to the wholesale food shop and decided to check on you on my way back." "Ah, my sister, we dey here o" Aunty Tina sighed. Leya arrived with a bottle of water and a glass. "Leya, how are you?" Reggie looked at Leya smiling. "I'm well Aunty Reggie. I hope you are doing okay too Ma" Leya asked as she poured the water for Aunty Reggie. "My dear, we can't complain" she replied, taking a sip of her water. Leya took the cup and went back to what she was doing. Tina's eyes trailed her, "Very lovely girl" she said. "Indeed!" Regina replied. "How far with what you told me?" Regina asked. "Hmm, you know business is still not doing well and my children have asked me to relocate and join them in Ghana. But my sister, each time I think

170

of Leya, I don't know what to do. This girl has been so good with my business since she arrived." Tina mentioned, turning to look at Leya. "I can have her" Aunty Regina offered. Tina looked at Regina, her eyes lighting up in excitement. "Hah, you mean it?" "Is this even a question? You know Gladys left to get married a few months ago and I have been looking for her replacement since." Tina smiled, heaving a sigh of relief. "Thank you God" she said looking at the ceiling briefly. "I couldn't bear to just put her out with no job. Thank you Reggie, Reggie. Somebody's heartbeat" Tina teased Reggie, patting her lap and playfully pushing her in the process. "Leave me jor" Aunty Reggie laughed.

"Let today be the start of something new" – Anonymous

Reggie's Bistro was located in the heart of the city centre giving easy access to the hungry shoppers and working class who flooded in and out every day. It had a cultural feel to it with beautiful African art placed strategically on the walls and a warm ambiance. The setting was brightly illuminated by African print chandeliers in various geometric shapes hanging beautifully on the ceiling. The tables were a dark walnut wood with soft comfortable grey chairs and tribal print runners. Placed on them were little candles effusing citron blossom cassis and Simi's music playing softly in the background. Reggie's bistro was a home away from home and this was evident in the customers who came and went in their numbers!

It was Leya's first day at work and as she sat across Aunty Reggie in a corner of the Bistro for her induction, away from any prying eyes, she looked around in admiration. "This place is so beautiful Aunty Reggie." "Ahhh, thank you! Born out of love, sweat and tears" she said looking around her Bistro with a look of content and pride. "Make yourself at home. I have seen your hard work whilst you were with Tina and I hope it reflects in your job here" she smiled. "Thank you Ma. I won't let you down." Leya replied. "Tina says you live quite farther away." "Yes ma" Leya said as her eyes turned briefly to the waitress busy attending to a customer. "I have a spare bedroom in my house. If you don't mind, you can move in there. Make it easier for you to get to work and attend your evening classes." Leya looked at Aunty Regina in shock, her eyes wide open. Once again, like a wounded soldier yet victorious on the battle field, the universe was smiling on her! This very attractive middle aged woman with a voluptuous body shape she admired, her hair always perfectly coiffed with grey streaks, was offering her abode. A woman she knew only as a friend to her former boss was offering her shelter just as Bunmi did a long time ago. She immediately fell to her knees in appreciation. "Thank you so much Ma. God bless you Ma, Thank you." "You're very welcome my dear." Aunty Regina smiled beckoning her to get up.

"It doesn't matter who hurt you or broke you down. What matters is who made you smile again" - Anonymous

Aunty Reggie's home was just as beautiful as the way she had designed her Bistro. It was a gated 3 bedroom detached bungalow with beautiful flowers growing in their pots placed a few inches apart from each other on the terrace. From her many travels, she had incorporated a piece of each memory in her home design which was a mix of both traditional and contemporary. Leya had been fascinated by every item she saw especially the picture of a man beautifully framed sitting on her ankara console table, a large round sunburst mirror on the wall and an orchid plant in a vase placed on the left. She wondered who he was and was certain he must have meant a lot to Aunty Reggie. *Maybe her husband or brother?* Leya thought. Aunty Reggie had been so good to her, treating her like a little sister that blew Leya's mind. This woman must have been a guardian angel sent by God to replace Bunmi, for she acted in ways so similar to Bunmi. Well, except for the brash, crazy character her Bunmi possessed. Aunty Reggie oozed some sort of class that could not be bought or learnt, it was innate. Leya enjoyed spending time with Aunty Reggie, listening to her stories from her travels in her spare time and cooking for her. She loved to cook and clean for her, it was the only way she could repay this lovely woman for her kindness. She had woken up early and was in the kitchen when Aunty Regina walked in. "Ahhh, I'm getting used to this o. Having someone around, keeping me company, helping my business and making me delicious meals" she said smiling, Leya laughed. "Good morning Aunty." "Morning my dear. Hope you slept well?" "Yes ma" Leya responded. "So what's for breakfast?" Aunty Regina asked, opening the bowls in excitement. "Some eggs, bacon, hash browns, mushrooms, tomatoes." Leya replied as Aunty Regina cut in, "Oohhh, a full English I see" she smiled. Her eyes caught Leya's scarred right hand. "Your right hand" she mentioned, looking at them intently, "What happened to it?"

Avoiding Aunty Reggie's gaze, she turned towards the pan, looking down and pretending to stir the mushrooms, "I had a bad fall." "Hmm." Aunty Regina replied unconvinced, catching the sudden sadness that engulfed Leya. She moved towards her, placing her hand on Leya's back, "You know you can always talk to me right?" She said concerned. "Yes, yes I know. I'm fine." Leya responded, trying to force a smile. "Now, let me get these done and then on to the bacon" she said, trying to avoid Aunty Regina's gaze. *Who could have hurt this lovely girl?* Aunty Reggie thought quietly as she watched Leya.

The sun had set! Darkness was upon the earth and the crickets sang, when Leya walked through the door. Aunty Regina reading a book, turned to look at her in a frown, "No night class today?" She asked. "No, teacher cancelled. Something about his wife going into labour." Leya responded, sitting down exhausted and flinging her bag on to the seat next to her. "You left the Bistro early today" she said to Aunty Reggie concerned. "Yes. I had a hospital appointment. Thought I told the girls to inform you." "They did. Is everything okay?" Leya asked, a look of worry on her face. "Everything is just fine." Aunty Reggie replied, smiling at Leya. "Just a routine check-up. I made us some dinner. Thought you might be hungry when you returned from night school." "If you had a hospital appointment, you should be resting not cooking Aunty." Leya gently chastised her. Aunty Regina had told her not call her "Ma" anymore and Aunty was just fine - she quite liked calling her Aunty. Aunty Regina laughed, "Ah ah, what are you now? My mother?" "Well, you've been so kind to me since the day you met me at Aunty Tina's fabric shop. You haven't stopped being nice to me. Taken me under your roof, given me a job. I could never repay you for this and I don't want anything to happen to you." Leya said almost in tears, overcome by emotion. "Heyyy" Aunty Regina said, moving towards her and sitting next to her. "I needed the company anyway. I mean, look at me, forty seven years old, no child, no husband. Well, I did have a husband, God rest his beautiful soul." she said, looking over to the picture of the man in the frame. "Was that him?" Leya asked. She had been waiting for this moment. Aunty Regina, still looking at the picture, her face in a smile that spelt beautiful memories, nodded. "Yes, that was him. Love of my life! It was almost like our souls were intertwined." She turned to look at Leya, "How come you never had kids?" Leya asked. Realising she had over stepped her boundaries, she quickly apologised. "Sorry, so sorry. That was insensitive. I should not have asked that?" "No, its fine." Aunty Regina said to her. "We did have a child, once, many years ago but we lost the baby at birth." "So sorry to hear that," Leya whispered. Aunty Regina let out a sad smile. "After that loss, we tried and tried but I guess the only child assigned to me by God was the one we lost. 3 miscarriages and 2 failed IVFs later, I lost hope and almost became a shadow of myself. To help me out of depression and take my mind off not being able to have any more children, we decided to set up a Bistro style eatery from our many travels." "When did your husband pass?" Leya asked quietly. "My soul mate left this earth almost 2 years ago and I miss him every single day." Aunty Regina said, looking over at the picture again. Leya bowed her head and for a flash moment, Jay crossed her mind. "Now, let's talk about you" Aunty Regina said smiling and looking at Leya. "Me?" Leya asked surprised. "Yes, you! Who are you really? Where are you from? I need to know more about the very beautiful young lady who shares my home. What if you're a convict running away from the authorities?" Aunty Reggie eyed her suspiciously, Leya laughed. "I am running, but not from authorities." Leya looked at Aunty Reggie, her eyes sad! "I'm all ears!" Aunty Reggie replied, taking Leya's hand in hers.

"A problem shared is a problem halved" – Proverbial Saying

15

"Accept what is, let go of what was, and have faith in what will be"- Sonia Ricotti

Jay and Dami's relationship had blossomed steadily. Their interests were very similar, spending their free time visiting the art galleries, attending TED talks, cocktail parties and generally enjoying each other's company. For some odd reason, the closest intimacy they shared was a cuddle, the occasional peck on the cheek and lots of hugs. A part of him held back – which was unlike him in the company of a woman like Dami. He was cautiously dipping his foot into the unknown and what this new relationship would bring, whilst intentionally holding back. Truth was, he felt by some miracle Leya might walk through his door one day. Then again, she had been gone for a year and over now and all his private investigation had brought no leads. It was probably time to close this chapter, accept his losses and move on.

Watching a series on the wide screen television in his living room, Dami lay on his chest as they cuddled up quietly engrossed in the show. The rhythm of his heart beat almost as soothing as listening to the quiet waves of the sea. She had fallen in love with this man! He was everything she imagined her partner to be. Raising her head to look at him for a few seconds, she thought to herself how gorgeous his eyes were as she moved closer to his face and kissed him gently on his lips. Surprised by her action, he had never imagined Dami to be one who made the first move. "What was that for?" He asked, a curious smile plastered all over his face. "For being the nicest, sweetest man I've ever met" She replied. "Since we began dating, you have never forced yourself on me or initiated an action that made me uncomfortable" she said, stroking his chest. "I want you Jay. I am attracted to you, mind and body, my body yearns for you inside of me" she whispered, turning to stroke his face gently. He liked a woman who knew what she wanted and was not afraid to show, her action turned him on. They glanced at each other for a moment that felt like they were floating, until she leaned closer for another kiss. He placed his lips on hers as he kissed her shivering lips. The anticipation, his intense passion, drove her to the edge as Jay pushed her slightly on to the sofa, arching himself over her as she lay on the sofa surrendering her body to him. His hands explored her body as he undressed her. If this was heaven, she was home!

The boys had gathered at Jay's house, which they did occasionally. It was their time to let their hair down and talk about the many life experiences they encountered. They had all been there for each other in trying times and this further sealed the brotherhood they shared. "So I'm like, can I buy you a drink and she responds, sorry, alcohol is bad for my legs. I look at her like what? And then I was like, what happens to your legs when you drink alcohol? Do they swell up or something? Chic looks me in the eye and says, no, they spread." Tayo said to the boys who laughed so hard, falling back into their chair. "Chic knows herself then" Fred said giggling. "Well, at that point, I wished she drank alcohol because man was horrrnyyyy" Tayo shouted. "Tayo, always sowing his royal oaths everywhere" Chuks said, pretending to look disgusted at his friend. "Errrr any one heard about the story of the pot, the kettle, black??" Jay asked as they continued to laugh. Amidst the laughter and hearty conversation, Dami came down the staircase in a floor length thin strap emerald green maxi dress with beautiful detailing at the bottom, her blow dried natural hair falling over her shoulders. The boys turned to look, stunned to see her around. "Ummm I see something's getting pretty serious here" Chuks muttered under his breath as Tayo nudged his side to shut him up. "Hi boys" she smiled walking over to them. "Hey Dami" they replied in unison as Fred looked on, keenly observing. She turned to Jay and smiled, he smiled back reaching to hold her by the waist. "Have you been here all weekend?" Chuks asked, Tayo nudged him again! "Yes" she replied, a shy look on her face. "I see!" Chuks responded, trying so hard not to chuckle. "Anyways, I'll leave you boys to it whilst I finish some office work" she said and turned to look at Jay, "Was wondering if you still wanted us to go out to dinner." Talking to him out of ear shot of the others. Jay nodded, "Yeah, when the boys leave." She smiled, kissing him lightly on the lips as the boys looked on before walking back upstairs. Tayo and Chuks began to tease Jay, "Guyyyyy, you're like the king of got it. You've just got it mehnn" Tayo playfully pushed Jay's arm.

"These ladies be eating outta your fingers all the time" Chuks continued, giving Jay a playful nudge. Shaking his head and pretending to ignore them, he sat on the sofa and picked up the TV remote oblivious of Fred's prolonged intense gaze on him as the others continued to tease. Then he knew! His cousin was still in love with the other girl!

"The most important thing in the world is family and love"
– John Wooden

Elena was happy! Her son had come back to her from his wallow of self-pity and the deep depression he sank into when Leya left. She had never seen him this way with any of the ladies he had dated and this prompted her to find out more about Leya. A part of her felt terrible for being hard on the young lady. It had become clear to her that in this case, love could be enough. In Leya's truth to her son, he had accepted her light and her darkness. However, it was a little too late now as just as magic, Leya had disappeared off the face of the earth with no trace at all. *Dami seemed like a good replacement*, she had thought. After all, Dami embodied the perfect wife material her son needed. "Dude, be honest. Do you love Dami or she's just a void you're trying to fill. Rebound maybe?" Fred asked Jay worryingly as they all relaxed in the beautiful large garden in Elena's house. The smell from the roses stirring their senses with their beautiful soft floral notes lingering in the air around them. "C'mon now, mummy dearest here once said to a girl I loved and lost that love was never enough. Right mom?" Jay said to his mum in a harsh sarcastic tone. "Olugbenga Daniels, I promise you, I don't care if you're now a big boy. If you speak to me just as you did a few seconds ago, I will slap out those demons affecting your senses." Elena retorted. Fred chuckled, careful not to let Elena see his face as he turned to look at his dad, Uncle Tyrone. "I'm sorry" Jay looked at her apologetically. "Now, to your question, yes, love is never enough. However, I understand there are exceptions to the rules and besides, it's been over a year now. Honey, if she was going to come back, she would have" Elena said just as Jay got up suddenly, exasperated. "I drove her away mum, you drove her away too!" "Me??" Jay's mum asked surprised. "...and you Fred!" he pointed to him. "What?" Fred asked, his face twisted in absolute confusion. "Yes! All of us. I expected the people I loved the most to back me up, my family. Damn it! It was only Uncle T here who genuinely liked her. Uncle T shifted and relaxed in his rattan chair with a proud look and a smirk on his face to the accused two. Our attitude, social conformity, everything! Why are we not allowed to just love who we want?" "You tell them boy! You tell them!" Uncle T exclaimed, interrupting Jay. They all turned to look at him, "Like, no disrespect to your mum" he said to Fred, "but if only they had just let me marry my Korean girl, Chan-Sook, I'd have been happily married but no! They said I had to marry Ajoke because she came from a family as ours. I mean, even her jollof tasted like sh…" Fred looked at his dad sternly, "…never mind" Uncle T muttered under his breath, looking away. "Really Tyrone" Elena said to her brother. "You'd have preferred eating Chan-Sook's jollof which tasted like, like it was made of just water and ketchup?" She asked. "Yes! It was a labour of love! And I'd have eaten it even if it turned into a pudding. Oh Chan-Sook, I always wondered what could have been" he responded to his sister dreamingly. Elena shook her head in defeat. "People find love in the most hopeless places, let the boy choose for himself who he wants" Uncle T said. Jay continued, "For Pete's sake, I broke an already broken girl. You did your investigations mum, you found out all she had been through." His mum sighed and got up, Fred stood up too. "So, are you going to spend the rest of your days feeling guilty about this?" She asked. "Fine, maybe, in one way or the other, we did push her away, but honey, it's happened, water under the bridge. Dami is a lovely girl, has a good head on her shoulders. Move on baby, move on." His mum put her right arm around him, that soothing comfort only a mother could elicit. "You hired a private investigator, got the police all out looking for her. They came back with nothing." Fred said. "Look, if I could bring her back to you, I would, but Jay, dude, the girl is gone. Where? God knows, but you've beaten yourself up about this for far too long." Jay sat back down, his head in his hands as he inhaled and exhaled deeply. Uncle T patted his back gently, reassuringly!

"When I close my eyes, I see you. When I open my eyes, I miss you" – Anonymous

16

"The only strategy that is guaranteed to fail is not taking risks" – Mark Zuckerberg

"We have surveyed the area, the land is perfect. Next step is get the architects in" the manager said, showing Jay some documents. The company had acquired a vast land in the most unfavourable part of the city plagued with lack of housing, water and non-existent electricity. Jay had gone for the land bid against the opposition from his mum and the board of directors and won. Through a SWOT analysis, he had managed to convince the board of the opportunities and business growth the project will bring, setting up a business continuity plan to manage this. Jay was a risk taker and this was his forte. He carefully went through the papers, his crisp white sleeves rolled up carelessly up his arm as he always did. "Good! Good head start" he said flipping through the documents. "When do we meet with the architects?" Jay asked. "They are on standby really, and just waiting for our call sir" The manager replied. "I would like to meet with them. We can't get this wrong." He dialled the office phone, "Priscilla, can you come in here for a second please" Jay instructed. Within seconds, Priscilla his assistant walked in clutching a note pad and a pen. "Cancel my meeting with the managers at the Point hotel, I need an 11am flight arranged." Priscilla scribbled away, "First or business class sir?" She asked. "C'mon Priscilla, you know this" he responded. She smiled and noted that down. "Ermm, arrange for my suit to be picked up from the dry cleaners." "Yes sir." She replied. "Call mum and reschedule our lunch date, explain I have to be with the architects ASAP to get the ball rolling for the real estate project launch and I'll call her when I arrive." "Okay Sir. Will that be all?" She asked. "Yes" he responded, signing a document on the table and handing it over to the manager. As she turned to leave, he called out, "Oh, and Priscilla," she turned. "Sir?" "Thank you for all your help," he smiled at her. Priscilla walked away blushing.

****

Jay all suited up, greeted the head of design at the door as they shook hands. "Mike Suleiman" Jay said. "Jay Daniels" he responded. "How was your flight?" Mike asked, walking Jay into the building and to the elevator leading to his office. "Pleasant" he replied, unbuttoning his blazer as he took a seat relaxing into it. "I'm actually glad you decided to come yourself, there have been a few adjustments to the design and we wanted to show this to you before anything else" as he passed a portfolio to Jay. Jay looked at them intently nodding his head. "I see we might need pillars to support the structure over here" he pointed as Mike stretched his head to look at what Jay was referring to. "We are looking to construct a geometric alignment to this structure" he pointed. "That way, we won't need pillars to support" he finished. "Great stuff! Man, are we taking a major business risk here, considering the area we want to undertake this project" Jay said handing the drawing back to Mike. "Every risk is worth it if it's for a good cause, and lives are going to be changed for the better" Mike assured him. "I guess" Jay shrugged his shoulders. "So, how long are you here with us for?" Mike asked. "A few days" Jay answered. "Not long enough to show you the beautiful sights of our city" he replied. "Unfortunately not. At least, this new project would mean I get to come over a few more times." Jay smiled. "Well," Jay said standing up "Been a long morning. Need to get some rest. I'll see you nice and early at the site?" He asked. "Sure thing. The team and I will be there." "Good, Mike" Jay said shaking his hand as he headed for the door.

****

Reggie's Bistro was in full buzz! Home-style cooked meals with their sweet aroma swirled around as waitresses went in and out of the kitchen holding mouth-watering dishes. In the back office, Leya sat behind the desk doing the accounts. She could not believe how far she had come each time she sat down behind the computer like a boss, checking the expenditure and profits. Aunty Reggie had trusted Leya so much from living with her that she had entrusted the day to day running of the business into her care for days when she was unavailable. Leya loved working for and living with Aunty Reggie. She had become like a big sister to her who advised her, genuinely cared and prayed with her. Leya had never been religious, especially after her childhood abuse and trauma that followed. She had resolved to tell herself there was no God and he was a figment of people's imagination. However, through Aunty Reggie's guidance and love, memories of Bunmi and all the people that had been placed in her life's path, she began to understand there was a force greater than met the eye. The best part of going to church with Aunty Reggie were the worship sessions. She revelled those moments, feeling an even deeper connection with God. Her spiritual journey was in its teething stage but she was loving every moment of knowing God, understanding the Trinity and as Aunty Reggie would always mention to her – baby steps! The only way she could repay this woman with a heart of gold was to ensure her business stayed afloat and successful.

Going through the menu list, Chioma walked in with her usual bubbly mood. "Second madam" she joked as Leya lifted her head up. "Chioma" Leya acknowledged, smiling and returning to her calculator. "What are you doing?" Chioma asked, stretching her neck and straining her big round eyes to look. Chioma had worked at the Bistro since she came to the city from the village 3 years ago. She was a full figured lady with a wandering eye that made her look constantly distracted. She loved her food and her double chin was a reflection of her good appetite. Leya had hit it off with her the moment they met and her personality, almost bearing a resemblance to Bunmi's made them get on like a house on fire. "Is Aunty Reggie not coming in today?" She asked. "She is, later" Leya responded, still focused on her calculations. "Ehen, I wanted....." Chioma began to talk when someone at the front shouted "Service." "Ah, we have customers" Chioma said as she headed out. "I'm coming, I have gist for you. Let me just go and take order first." Leya looked at her, shaking her head at Chioma's all too familiar antics. She smiled and said to her, "I'll be waiting for this gist." Chioma walked into the main eating area, going over to attend to the customers seated at the table. Spotting Mike Suleiman, she let out a wide grin "Oga Mike. How far now?" "Madam Chiom Chiom, I dey like Dele" he replied. Noticing the well-dressed, classic gentleman sitting next to Mr Suleiman, she gave a flirtatious smile. "Welcome to Reggie's Bistro, my name is Chioma and I'm at your service today. May I take your order" she asked. Jay looked at Mike, "You know what you're having? Cuz I'm spoilt for choice here." Mike let out a short laugh, "See? I told you. Reggie's Bistro is one of the best eateries we have here in town. Their meals taste like food you'll eat from home I tell you." Mr Suleiman picked up the menu, glancing through, he said, "I'm going to try the crispy sesame chicken for starters, some yam and sweet plantain porridge for the main." Chioma smiled and wrote it down. "..And you sir?" she asked looking at Jay blushing. "I think I'll just have what my man here is having, thanks." "Okay sir. Any drinks? We make the best zobo in town." Jay looked at the menu again and said, "I think I'll just have a regular coke please?" "Sure." Chioma replied looking at him, her jaws hurting from smiling so much. Jay smiled back at her. "I think I'll just stick with coke too" Mike agreed. "Okay, if that's everything, your order will be with you shortly" Chioma said as she walked away swaying her hips and hoping Jay noticed her most acknowledged feature – her big bum. She handed the order to the kitchen staff and ran back into the office almost out of breath. "Are you okay?" Leya asked looking at her concerned. "Chaiiiiii, you need to come and see the fine specimen of a man whose order I have just taken" Chioma replied. Leya tilted her head back laughing. "So, it is fine boy that is doing you like this?" Leya asked, teasing her. "This one is not ordinary o. See face, see height, see cloth, see charisma, see voice on top foreign accent, infact ehnnn, see everything! Some people can fine sha" she continued, gesturing with her hands. Leya still laughing, said to her, "What fine boy will do to you. Abeg leave me, let me sort out Aunty Reggie's stock jor," returning to her paperwork. "Leya nowwwww, come and just peep" Chioma said beckoning Leya. "Chioma leave me alone o. You sef know say your exaggeration no get part two. I'll go now and see one kind gbonyo looking face." Leya giggled sitting down and picking up her sheet. "Let me go and serve them their food first" Chioma said as she walked out the door again. Leya looked at her walking away, nodded her head and smiled.

After Chioma served the food before them, the men said thank you, tucking in. She walked back to the little office, her face dreamy, "I can even smell the guy's money from a distance." Chioma said, playfully twisting the strands of the single box braids on her head. "Chioooma! Ah ah," Leya laughed. "This guy must drop his number for you before he leaves o" Leya continued, looking at Chioma. "Forget! Me sef know say him level pass my own, so let me just admire from a distance abeg. I no wan wahala." For a split moment, Leya was overcome with sadness as her mind filled with memories of her disrupting Jay's work on his laptop and in his frustration, chasing her around his beautiful home until he got hold of her, kissing her with so much passion in his veins. She had blanked him from her mind completely, *but why was he suddenly often creeping into her head these days*, she thought to herself. Chioma spotted her sudden demeanour, "Are you okay?" she asked. Leya turned to her, smiled and said, "Yes, I'm okay. Okay, let me finish this last stock inventory and I will come out and see the customer that has mesmerized you." Chioma laughed and walked back to the main hall. At this point, Jay and Mike had finished their meal. She went over to them, "Everything alright?" She asked. "Food was great thanks" Jay acknowledged. "Chiom Chiom, can we have the bill please?" Mike asked, toothpick in his mouth. Chioma walked away to bring the bill and quickly went back door to Leya, "Hurry o, they're leaving." Leya laughed. "It is well o Chioma, it is well. Let me just put this up on the shelf." "Okay," Chioma said excitedly and walked out. After finally sorting out Aunty Reggie's stock and expenditures, Leya walked out, looking around the Bistro. "Ah, where are they?" she asked. Chioma looked her up and down in a frown, "Question! They left." She responded, kissing her teeth. "Come and see, come and see, you were forming chief accountant inside" she continued. Leya burst into laughter, "No vex now. I had to finish stock taking," trying to appease Chioma. "He sha tipped me wella" flashing her money notes. "That's a lot of tip o" Leya looked at her amazed as she tried to take the money away from Chioma. Chioma moved her hand back in playful aggression, "Ehn ehn, comot your hand from my money o. When Oga Mike comes back, you can collect your own" she said, putting the money in her pocket. "Oga Mike?" Leya asked. "Yes na! He came with the other bobo" Chioma replied. "He liked our service and the food, so he said he will come back again when next he is in town. E be like say he is not from around, maybe na obodo oyibo guy" Chioma continued, moving over to clear the plates from the table. Leya looked at her and shook her head. "Chioma of life!!! You remind me so much of someone I know." Chioma looked at Leya frowning, "Ah! Impossible o, there can only be one Chioma in this life. No one before, no one after" Chioma exclaimed, Leya laughed.

17

"If music be the food of love, play on" – William Shakespeare

It was Leya's day off from work, and as she sat on the sofa with one of Aunty Reggie's legs on her lap, she massaged her foot. "How's night school coming along?" Aunty Reggie asked. "Well, picking up a lot, learning a lot and I am actually proud of myself" Leya said smiling. "Well, you should be" Aunty Reggie replied. "You're turning your lemons into lemonade and doing a damn good job at it" wincing at a slight discomfort from the foot rub. Aunty Reggie had been so easy to talk to and non-judgemental about Leya's past that she had wished she also told her about her rapes. However, she did not want to relive the pains of her past

197

and decided her childhood be left with the only two people who knew her story. "Here?" Leya asked, looking at the spot the discomfort came from. "Yes, there." Aunty Reggie confirmed. Leya continued to massage her foot as Aunty Reggie suddenly asked, "Do you miss him?" The question caught Leya off guard completely as she suddenly stopped the massage. "Have you ever thought of giving Jay a call?" Aunty Reggie continued. Leya went back to massaging the foot, "No. It's been too long now. He must have moved on. Besides, if I truly mattered to him, he would have tried to find me." "How do you know he never did?" Aunty Reggie asked. "He may have done, he may not have. All in the past now." Leya said, avoiding Aunty Reggie's gaze. "Is it really?" Aunty Reggie asked, Leya looked at her!

The afternoon was really hot and humid, Jay sat in the air conditioned office with Mike Suleiman and the team as they finalised all plans. They had sorted out everything they required to move on to the next phase of the project which was building construction. "I guess this is it" Jay pointed out, as they all clapped in excitement. "We cannot wait to showcase a masterpiece in this city" Mike responded, shaking hands with Jay. "What time is your flight scheduled for?" "7pm. Why?" Jay asked as the rest of the staff began to walk out of the office. "I wanted to treat you to some delicious peppered fish" Mike said. Jay laughed, "I think I have time for some delicious peppered fish." "Trust me, you'll be licking your lips and wanting to return to Abuja" Mike assured him as they both walked out of the office. "They should make you minister for food tourism." Jay said to Mike who tilted his head back in laughter.

"The pain of parting is nothing to the joy of meeting again"
– Charles Dickens

Jay and Mike Suleiman were seated with a drink at the Bistro when Aunty Reggie walked over to them. "Aunty Reggie!" Mike exclaimed, standing up to give her a warm hug. "Mike Mike, big Mike. How are you now?" She asked. "Very well. See as you're looking fresh by the day" Mike said, admiringly. She let out a beautiful warm laugh as Jay looked on at her. "It's God o" She replied. "I don't see you here as often" Mike mentioned. "I know, got some good girls here who manage this place well, even in my absence. That way I can go about my other business." "Business woman of life!" Mike replied, giving her accolades. She laughed again, her gaze drawn to Jay. "You look familiar" she said smiling. He stood up to greet her, bowing in respect. *Charming young man*, Aunty Reggie thought to herself. "That's Mr Jason Daniels, Aunty Reggie. He's in our city for a business project. This man is about to create affordable state of the art housing for the masses." Mike said, gently patting Jay's shoulder. She shook his hands smiling, "Welcome to Reggie's Bistro." "You have such a beautiful place here" Jay replied, looking around and back at her. "Ahhhh, thank you. Make yourself at home and I'll get one of the girls to come take your order." "Thank you. This is actually my second visit" Jay said sitting back down. "Oh, really? Well, I appreciate the love coming back" Aunty Reggie smiled at him as she walked back into the office. "We have customers, can you go and take their order" Aunty Reggie said to Leya as she counted packs of drinks with Chioma. Chioma quickly dropped the paper and pen in her hand, "I'll go." Aunty Reggie stopped her with her hand. "No! Leya, you go. Chioma can finish taking the drinks stock." "Aunty, I don't mind doing the stock if Chioma wants to go" Leya told her. "Chioma does not like taking stock, let her learn. You go!" Aunty Reggie scolded as Chioma frowned playfully. Leya giggled, handing her paper to Aunty Reggie and then walking out as Aunty Reggie playfully hit Chioma's head with the paper, "Oya, back to stock taking. Quick quick."

Leya walked over to the table, her face lighting up as she saw Mike. "Ahhh Mr Suleiman. Long timeee" she stressed. He got up, gave her a quick hug and said to her smiling, "Leyaaa, beautiful, beautiful Leya. How now?" "I'm well o. I haven't seen you in a while. You've found a new eatery abi?" She frowned as he laughed out loud. "No now! Never! Aunty Reggie's Bistro for life until I marry" he said. "Even when you marry, you still have to come here o." Giggling, he said to her, "I was here the other day." "Ehnnn?" She responded. "Yeah, I was. Came with a client but I figured you might have been off that day or probably in the back office busy. As a matter of fact, he is here again with me today. I wanted him to taste your special peppered fish before his flight." Leya laughed, "Thank you for the recommendation o, should I just go get the order or wait for....." "....he's just gone to take a call outside." Mike interrupted, Leya looked around. "Oh, here he comes," Mike pointed over to Jay walking towards them. Leya turned to look, her eyes and mouth froze in shock surprise just as Jay walked up to her equally speechless. They stood staring at each other unblinking, different waves of emotions flowing through their bodies as time stopped around them. Leya could feel her legs shaking, she felt paralysed as her knees became weak. Jay's heart was beating faster than a drummer at a concert. He appeared startled, this could not be real, for it was as seeing the sunlight after many months of rain. Here she was again, standing right before him, the woman he spent endless nights thinking about! For what felt like eternity, their eyes locked with each other's. Mike Suleiman cleared his throat giggling, jolting Jay and Leya back to reality. "Ss sorry, ermmm, mm my my name is Le, Leya, welcome to auntie's, I mean Reggie's Bistro. Mm, may I take your order?" her brain stuttered looking at him. Jay grabbed the menu, "Ermmmm, ehhh" appearing confused. Mike looked at him breaking down in laughter, "Jay, you're looking at the menu upside down." Jay looked at the menu and realised he was indeed reading it upside down, turning it the other way round. "I'll eh, I'll..." Mike cut in, "We'll have the peppered fish please." Leya nodded and walked away, her body shivering! Jay sat quiet for a while, "Are you okay?" Mike asked smiling. "You've been left dumbfounded after seeing fine girl abi?" he laughed. Jay looked at him sternly, "This girl, Leya. How long has she been working here?" he asked. "For a long time now" Mike answered. "We didn't see her the last time" Jay stated. "Yeah, she must have been busy at the back office or at school." "School?" Jay asked, his brows raised. "Yes, I think she studies as well. Is everything okay? You like her? Very normal for Leya now. Every time I'm here, the guys try to make a pass at her. Very lovely girl in and out, so don't worry, normal level." Mike Suleiman teased Jay.

Leya stood behind the kitchen door, taking deep breaths. She was having panic attacks and could not breathe. "Are you okay?" Chioma asked Leya concerned. "Yes, yes, I'll, I'm fine I'm fine" she responded out of breath, quickly gathering the order as it was given to her by the kitchen staff. "This your, I'm, I'll, you sure say you dey okay?" Chioma asked just as Aunty Reggie entered. She looked at Leya and said gently, "Your customers are waiting." Leya gathered herself "Yes, sure Aunty." Aunty Reggie looked on at her, a warm smile on her face as Leya walked past her towards the table, her hands visibly shaking. She got to the table and as she placed the order before Jay, her hands let go, spilling part of the sauce on his shirt. "I'm sorry, I'm so sorry" she apologised to him, taking a napkin. As she stretched to wipe the stain off his shirt, he placed his hand over hers. A warm sensation flowed through her body, a beautiful sweet memory. He looked at the scar on her hand, gently brushing his thumb over it and then said to her in an almost whisper, "It's only a stain. It's fine." She nervously moved her hand from his and said, "I'll ermm, I'll bring you another plate." "No, honestly, its fine." His beautiful eyes locked with hers, staring. She nodded and walked away as quickly as her legs could carry her. Mike looked at both of them confused, he smiled shaking his head as he tucked into his grilled peppered fish.

Leya was pacing up and down the kitchen when Aunty Reggie walked in. She turned to look at Aunty Reggie, her face shrouded in shock and worry, "You knew!" she said anxiously. Aunty Reggie smiled, nodding her head. Walking over to Leya, she took her in her arms and gave her a warm embrace before saying to her, "Not initially. I was just admiring the fine young man before me until his name was mentioned and all I could do was try to hide my surprised look. Besides he did look familiar." "I can't do this!" Leya said on the verge of tears. Aunty Reggie placed her hands on Leya's shoulders. "Yes you can. Now, be brave, go out there and attend to him, for some destinies are written in the stars."

Leya walked back to the table after their meal. "I hope you enjoyed your meal?" She asked calmly and better composed, avoiding Jay's intense gaze on her. "It was goooood, as usual." Mike said getting up and slightly rubbing his round belly. Jay placed a huge tip on the table as Mike looked at him unfazed by his action. "For your kind service," he said to Leya who looked at the money, before briefly looking at him and nodding in appreciation. As Mike began to converse with Leya, Jay walked away from them pulling his phone out of his trouser pocket. He dialled a number and put the phone to his ears, "Cancel my flight for tonight Priscilla, I'll let you know when to reschedule."

*"**When love is real, it finds a way" – Avatar Roku: The Last Airbender***

18

"He is her strength, she is his weakness and together their love was magic" – N.R Hart

Leya's mind was busy! The day's event kept playing in her head and it seemed so unreal. It had been over a year and she thought she had gotten over him until she lay her eyes on him once again. He looked just as handsome as the first day she met him, although it looked like he had lost a little weight and his eyes appeared tired. He was so close to her yet so far as she lay on the bed restless. Still battling to sleep, she got up, looked out her window. The night was quiet as the stars came out in their numbers like a perfect choir, its bright lights singing in beautiful patterns that adorned the sky. She went back to lie down again, her eyes opened, staring at the ceiling and watching the fan swirl. Never did she think she was going to see him again, and now there was that unshakeable feeling of care flooding through her body like a rushing lake – she was still hopelessly in love with him. Leya continued to watch the ceiling fan go round in circles when Aunty Reggie's deep coughs alarmed her and she rushed to her bedroom. "Aunty, are you okay? Can I get you some water?" she asked worried. Aunty Reggie said amidst her cough "I'm okay my darling. Yes, please get me some water." Leya ran to get her some water and brought it back. She took a sip, "You were not asleep?" She asked. Leya nodded, "I couldn't sleep." Aunty Reggie smiled. "The best love is the kind that awakens the soul, makes you restless until you have reached out to that someone." "I don't know if he feels the same way about me." "Even a blind man can see the affection he has for you. Annnnd he's very handsome." Aunty Reggie teased, poking Leya in the rib. Leya flinched, lowering her head in a blush. Aunty Reggie coughed again and Leya handed her the glass of water. "Thank you." she replied.

Jay lay in his bed at the hotel unable to sleep. Recounting the day's event was the most unexpected surprise he had ever had.

Leya looked just as beautiful as the day he met her fighting with Bayo, he smiled at the memory! She had gained a little weight in all the right places which made her look more enticing than ever. He had been mesmerized by her sheer beauty and even more proud that she had turned her life around and taken charge of it. He felt restless! She had always been on his mind and seeing her today made it worse. Jay turned to look at the bed side alarm, it showed 2.35am. He lay on the bed for a few seconds and got up. Walking around and staring out the window for a few minutes, he walked over to the table, opening his laptop and turning it on to do some work when his phone rang. He stared at it, Dami was calling. "Heyý" he said. "Hi baby" she responded. "You're still awake?" she asked. "Yeahhhh" Jay stressed, rubbing his head and eyes simultaneously, "Couldn't sleep so I figured I'll do some work until I fell asleep." "You poor thing. You work too hard. I miss you though, I miss you next to me. Your body next to mine." She said seductively as Jay remained silent. "I ermmm, I've got one or two things to wrap up over here and I'll be back in Lagos." he said eventually. "Hurry! My body yearns for you." Jay was quiet again. "Oh, I had lunch with your mum yesterday" Dami said to him. "You did?" He was not the least bit concerned or interested, he was just trying to make conversation. "Yes" Dami replied excitedly. "She's so lovely. We had an amazing time." "I bet!" Jay continued. "Okay, let me leave you now. Try and get some sleep babe" "I will," he responded. "I love you." Dami said. Speechless, he blurted out, "See you soon Dami." She hung up smiling whilst he looked at his phone and then rubbed his eyes.

It was just another busy day at Aunty Reggie's Bistro. The girls were going about their day when Jay walked in looking dapper in his light wash jeans, well steamed white oxford shirt and a deep navy suede blazer with his signature style of either rolling or pushing the sleeves carelessly up his elbows. They all rushed towards him like pack of flies, each trying to be at his service. "Hi" he said to them. "Is Leya working today?" Chioma walked over, giving the girls a reprimanding look as they began to scurry away. "Hello sir." She greeted smiling. "Hi, ermmm, is Leya around?" He asked. "Yes sir she is. Please take a seat and I'll call her" gesturing towards a seat for Jay as she turned to walk away, Jay stood! Chioma went to the back office to find Leya sorting out new glasses from their boxes. "Hmmmm, Prince charming is here o." Chioma teased. "Prince who?" Leya asked confused.

"Prince charming now. The guy who gave me that big tip the other day. The one who came here with Oga Mike." Leya frowned as her heart raced, "What does he want?" "Ah, me I don't know o but he has asked for you sha" Chioma winked. "For me?" Leya stood up and walked out as Chioma followed. She approached Jay, "I've been told you want to see me?" Her face stern. "Yes" Jay said looking at her, the kind that always made her feel uncomfortable in a warm way. "Is there a place we can talk?" He asked. "No, there's no place. I'm sorry, this is my job. You can't just come here wanting to talk. There are....." Jay cut in, "I know and I'm sorry to have just popped up at your workplace but I had no choice. I don't know where you live? I don't have your number? I just really needed to talk to you." Leya turned to Chioma standing next to her, smiling like a fool. "Please excuse us." Leya said to her. "Eh?" Chioma asked. "I said excuse us!" Leya raised her voice at her in frustration. "Ah, ah, calm down now. No be fight." Chioma responded. "Please Chioma." Leya said gently, her face in a plea. Chioma smiled and walked away. Leya led Jay to a corner seat where he gestured for her to sit first, pulling out her chair before he sat down. He stared at her for a while as they sat down silent for seconds. "How are you?" Jay finally asked. "I've been okay" she answered, avoiding his gaze. "God, you have no idea how it makes me feel seeing you again. Seeing you right before me, I miss you. Your voice, your smell, your jokes and silliness. I miss how you made me feel" Jay smiled at her. "I miss us!" He whispered. She looked at him briefly before looking away, she couldn't bear to look at those eyes which always captivated her in the most alluring way. She missed him too, more than he knew. "I thought you left for Lagos." she said. "No, cancelled my flight." he replied. She finally looked at him with a concerned look on her face, "Why?" He glanced at her for a few seconds in silence before responding, "You know why!"

"Can't fight this feeling" – Anonymous

The girls had wrapped up for the evening, Leya locked up the Bistro as the girls said their goodbyes. "See you tomorrow God willing" said Chioma, clutching the Bistro take away bag. Leya looked at her, "Come, what are you holding?" She asked. Chioma looked at her hand and the take away bag, "Food of course. Benefits of working in an eatery. No cooking for me and Bobo tonight. We are going to enjoy ourseffss." Leya laughed, nodding her head. "Chioma chop chop! Ah, ah!" Just at that moment, Jay walked over to meet them. "Good evening ladies" he said. "Mr Daniels" Chioma exclaimed with a wide grin, turning to look at Leya. "What are you doing here?" Leya asked. "I got a hire car, fancy taking a drive with me?" He coaxed. "I don't...." Leya began when Chioma quickly interrupted, "Yes!" Jay turned to look at her and chuckled. "Would you like a lift home too Chioma?" "Yesso, let me save my bus money abeg" she responded excitedly, walking past Jay and Leya towards the car and admiring it. Jay looked at Leya, taking her hand. Oh, how she missed his touch! "C'mon, please." "Oya now, you people" Chioma shouted holding the door handle, "My bobo dey wait o." "Her bobo dey wait o" Jay repeated to Leya who tried so hard not to laugh as she walked towards the car with his hand holding hers.

****

"Thank you sir" Chioma expressed excitedly, getting out of the car as they arrived at her house. "Please ehnn, if you're free tomorrow evening, you can come same time to the Bistro. We normally finish around...." "Chioma!" Leya exclaimed, interrupting her. "What?" Chioma asked, her face intentionally innocent. Jay giggled! "Have a good evening Chioma. Regards to your bobo" he mentioned. "Thank you Mr Daniels" she replied, winking at Leya. Chioma waved as they drove off and turned towards her compound gate. The drive to Aunty Reggie's home was in dead silence with Jay occasionally stealing glances at Leya. His Leya! She played with her fingers nervously, forcing a smile on Jay's face as he looked ahead driving. He knew Leya stuttered or played with her fingers when she was nervous. Jay cleared his throat, his car finally parked in Aunty Reggie's home. "So, I guess it's, good night?" He said looking at her. He wanted to kiss her so bad, feel her lips once again, hold her in his arms and never let go. She turned to look at him, this was the best feeling ever, sitting right next to the only man she ever loved. Her body screamed in glee within her, as she prayed for all the self-control she could get, so not to pounce on him and kiss him till the morning broke. "Yes, I guess" she responded shyly. As she turned to open the door, he caught her hand. "Please, stay here with me. You don't have to speak to me but just, stay." She let go of the handle as they sat in silence, his hand holding hers, placed on her lap. The only sound around them coming from the

90's RnB songs playing on the stereo. Jay squeezed Leya's hand gently when suddenly K-ci & Jojo's *"All my life"* began to play. This was their song! Danced to, many times back in Lagos. He stared at her deeply - their eyes explaining what their lips could not!

"A perfect night, few words spoken! Yet in our hearts, we knew." – Pookie Sho

It was the morning after! She had enjoyed listening to artistes as *Babyface, Luther Vandross, Michael Bolton, All 4 One, Whitney Houston, Mariah Carey, Shai, Boys2men, Celine Dion,* belting out tunes that was sweet melody to their ears and heart. They had sat in the car until the wee hours when Jay left, their only physical contact, the hands they held. They had said very little, yet there was so much they wanted to say to each other. For the first time in many nights, Leya slept well, waking up later than usual.

Leya was in the kitchen when Aunty Reggie strode in, "Good morning Aunty" Leya said, her face lit up in a radiant glow. Aunty Reggie walked over to the fridge, pouring herself a glass of cranberry juice and propping her body by the kitchen table watching Leya in silence and smiling. Leya made a face at her,

"Someone is happy?" Leya enquired. "Should I not be?" Aunty Reggie asked, taking a sip of her juice. "Everyone deserves to be happy" Leya answered. "So why are you denying yourself of this happiness?" Aunty Reggie asked. Before Leya could speak, she continued, "I watched a car drive in last night, I drew the curtains to check who it was and saw you both." Leya's face turned into embarrassment, "Sorry Aunty, I should not be bringing any one to....." Aunty Reggie cut in "You have never brought anyone here. No friends, no one. I'm not angry. In fact, I was glad." "It is out of respect to you. You have taken me in and I would never take your kindness for granted." Leya said to her. Aunty Reggie smiled, "I told you I needed the company. You've taken away the loneliness. Loneliness is such an evil thing sha." She chuckled and continued, "All I'm saying is, give him a chance to redeem himself." Leya nodded. "By the way, I think you two sitting in silence was the most romantic thing I've seen since my honey passed" she mentioned walking out of the kitchen, her back to Leya who smiled.

"A kiss is a lovely trick designed by nature to stop speech when words become superfluous" – Ingrid Bergman

The afternoon was unusually raw and cold, the sky filled with dark grey clouds that made for a lazy lie in. Jay had arrived back at his hotel in the early hours of the morning and had to catch up on some e-mails before going to bed. He lay in the comfort of his hotel bed dozing off after waking up briefly to brush his teeth and have some quick breakfast, when his phone rang. He picked it up with a muffled "Hello" half asleep. "Olugbenga, you're still sleeping at mid-day?" "Hey mum" he said. "Hi hun" Elena replied. "How come you are still asleep? Shey osu la' nor ni?" *Did you not sleep last night?* His mum asked in their local dialect. "Have you been running the clubs in Abuja?" "Nooo, no mum. I was working late" he said, eyes still closed. "Don't over work yourself my baby. You are indeed your father's son, always working. I hope the food is good at the hotel?" his mum continued just as he heard a knock on the door. He raised his head, face in a frown as he heard the door knock again. He wasn't expecting anyone and he would have been notified by the front desk if someone was here to see him. Walking over to open the door, he stood there eyes wide open in shock. "I'll call you back mum" hanging up the phone before Elena could say another word. "Come, come on in. Please" his voice nervous as Leya walked through the door, her midnight black hair falling seductively over her shoulder in a side part covering a bit of her face. She was wearing a black buttoned, sheer tulle polka dot mini dress with a collar. It's belt wrapped around her defined waist in a knot and the bottom part flowing freely high above her knees, revealing beautiful supple thighs. The click of her heels moved with rhythm, her soft curves visible through the inner thin vest of the dress as her eyes scanned the room. He moved quickly before her and started clearing the papers from his bed. "I erm, I wasn't expecting anyone" he said. "You always stay in these big big hotels" she replied, still looking around. He let out a short laugh, "There's nothing big about this hotel." "Nothing big about this place? Look at your big bed, nice looking things all around and it's no big deal to you? You these rich people sef" rolling her eyes, as she sat at the edge of the bed admiring the state of the art furniture and room decor. Jay chuckled, this was the Leya he knew! He stared at her admiringly, strong muscular arms folded across his bare chest, revealing the sculpted body she loved to trail her fingers over. "God, I missed you," he said, leaning on his table looking at her in a smile, his voice low and husky. Leya tried to avoid his intense gaze and naked top staring right in her face. The room was filled with an awkward, tensed silence, a burning passion waiting to erupt like magma filling the surface of a volcano. Jay broke the silence, "Your colleague Chioma, she reminds me of Bunmi." Leya giggled, "Yes, I always tell her that she reminds me of a dear friend. How is she by the way? Do you ever see her?" Leya asked. "I do actually. She's doing well, set up a Buka style restaurant playing the madam that she is." Leya laughed, "I'm so glad to hear that." "She misses you, you know." "I miss her too, very much. I left my phone in a hurry and I'm terrible with memorizing numbers." Leya replied. "So, what brings you here and how did you get past front desk without having them call me?" He asked. "I have my ways" she tilted her head to the side seductively. "You do huh" he responded, moving towards her just as his phone rang. He turned to look and it was Dami. Ignoring the call, he sat next to Leya on the bed. She shifted nervously, "You nervous?" he asked quietly as his hands moved to touch hers, watching his fingers trail up her arm. His phone rang again, "I think you need to pick that call. Whoever it is, is not going to stop." He sighed and picked it up, "Hi babe" Dami said. "Heyyy" he replied, moving away from Leya. "I'm missing you terribly. Like, so bad I had to come see you." "You what?" Raising his voice shocked and turning briefly to look at Leya who stared at him concerned. "You're what?" He asked again, this time his voice low. "I'm at the front desk of the hotel, come get me" Dami said. Jay laughed uncomfortably, "You're in Abuja? And at this hotel?" "Yep! Your mum gave me all the details. She was going to call you. Oh my God! Did she not call you? Have I bothered you?" Dami asked worried. "No! No, ermmm, mum tried to call me but I....." just then Leya got up to leave. "Dami, I need to call you back in a few minutes" he hung up and ran to hold her arm, stopping her. "Where are you going?" She looked at him, a sad smile all over her beautiful face. "It's taken me so long to get over you. Well, not really" she confessed, Jay's face lit up at her confession. "I tried to find my feet, which I did. I don't want to go back there again." She said quietly, almost on the verge of tears. "No, no, please listen" Jay said blocking her way. "Dami is a friend." "A friend?" She asked, raising her eye brows. "Jay, a friend would not come all the way here to see you" Leya said as she tried to move him away from the door. "No, no! I'm not going to do this with you" he said. "Do what?" she asked. "You're not going to leave until I explain" he shouted in frustration. "When you left, I searched everywhere for you. I hired a private investigator to find you, he came back with nothing. It was almost like you had disappeared off the face of the earth. I was lost without you. I couldn't even function well and I shut out everyone, blaming myself for what happened. I cut all ties with Amara, she moved to Canada. Then, as time went on and I realised you were gone forever, I started to get myself together. Went out with the boys one day and I met Dami" he explained. "You move on pretty quick don't you?" Leya said. Jay moved over to her and just as he was about to say something, they heard the door knock. "Your Dami might be at the door." Pretending not to have heard Leya nor the knock, Jay looked at her intently, his beautiful almond shaped eyes, staring deeply into hers. He tilted his head towards her face as she began to take deep breaths in anticipation, her eyes closed. His lips touched hers, they tasted of sweet succulent honey. He moved his head down to kiss her neck and shoulder. His tongue tracing the lines on her neck. "Jay....." her voice wavered. "Sshhhh" he whispered, his lips caressing her neck. "I'm so in love with you" Jay muffled between her shoulders as he moved his lips to hers, kissing her, passionately, as though through her, he got his air. He missed her, and his untamed passion reflected in the way he caressed her curves, opening the buttons of her dress and sliding his hand into her bra as he cupped her soft, ample breast. His hands played with her nipple in a way that drove her wild with intense desire. Leya kissed him back, her hands all over his body as she felt his hard bulge pressing against her body. Jay carried her, her arms and legs wrapped around him, each kiss fiery and wildly passionate. Their breaths mingled as each kiss and warm caresses, in their throes of passion, brought their bodies and soul together once again. The knock from the door became incessant, this time a lot harder and louder. "Argghhhh" Jay yelled out irritated, rubbing his head in frustration as he stopped and stared at Leya. His eyes apologetic, he put her down and went to open the door. Dami stood at the door, puppy faced. "You were taking so long to come get me, a staff showed me up here" she said. "I had to deal with something very important. Dami, we...." she hugged him before he completed his words, eyes closed. "I missed you so much." Feeling the hard bulge from his arousal between her crotch, she smiled, unaware of Leya who walked past them before Jay could stop her.

19

"If love is as sweet as a flower, then my mother is that sweet flower of love" – Stevie Wonder

Aunty Reggie's house had turned into a lovers squabble as Jay argued with Leya in her living room. She looked on in an all too familiar manner. "If you didn't matter to me, you think I'll be here and not with Dami at the hotel?" Jay asked raising his voice. "I don't even know why I came there" Leya said. "I'm so stupid. So stupid." "So missing someone and having the courage to let them know is stupid?" Jay asked "Then I'm stupid too." Leya stared at him. "I love you Leya, I loved you from the moment I heard your conversation in the elevator. I wondered who this feisty beautiful girl was and I was drawn to her. You complete me in a way no one has ever done. I'm crazy about you." he said to her, his arm stretched, holding hers. Aunty Reggie smiled, walking to the kitchen. "Dami?" Leya asked as Jay wrapped his arms around her, her head resting on his chest. "I'll sort that out." he said. "Here we go again." Leya said frustrated as she let go of him, walking towards the kitchen. "What?" Jay followed her. "Did you sort Amara out Jay? No. You told me how much you wanted me but you still let her come into your house, into your bed wearing just a robe. Remember?" Her voice raised as she entered the kitchen, Jay behind her. Aunty Reggie turned to look at them as she took some plates out from the cupboard for dinner. Jay asked, "What's that got to do...." Leya interrupted him, raising her arms high up in frustration, "Is this Dami issue not similar to....." Aunty Reggie screamed, the plates in her hands dropping to the floor, crashing into pieces. "Aaahhhhhhh" she screamed holding her tummy, they rushed to hold her. She looked at Leya in despair, "Ahhhhhh, God! God! Goddd!" she shouted. "Jay and Leya looked at each other confused, "What's wrong?" Jay asked, a look of worry on his face. Aunty Reggie looked at Leya, "What's your name?" She asked frantically. Jay looked at Leya confused once again. "Aunty, my name is Leya. Aunty you're making me worried" "No! No! What's your name? What's your real name?" Aunty Reggie shouted, her body in a shiver and still muttering "God! God! God." She held Leya's hands, "What's your real name? What name did you have at the orphanage?" Leya let go of Aunty Reggie's hand in shock, staring at her totally stunned. How did she know about the orphanage? They had never discussed past her relationship with Jay and her former life as a prostitute. Completely mesmerised, Leya began to mention her real name, "Fa..." Aunty Reggie interrupted her, "Fa'izah." They stared at each other transfixed! Aunty Reggie raised her arm showing the same inscription Leya had. "This inscription! I was marked with this at birth. I marked my baby girl before she was taken away from me with the same inscription that, that someday, maybe someday, I will find her again. Where's your locket? I gave you my locket." Leya covered her mouth with her hand, this could not be real! Jay looked on in utter shock. "Fa'izah, my Ifedimma, you came back to me, God. Thank you, thank you. Daalu, Daalu ooo" Aunty Reggie screamed, lying and rolling on the floor overcome with emotion as she cried out, "She came back to me, you heard my cry. God, you heard my cry. My baby has come back to me. Fa'izah! Fa'izah my child, my baby is home, my child is home!" Leya burst into tears as she wrapped her arms around the woman she had known only as Aunty Reggie, on the floor. They hugged each other crying, Jay rubbed his eyes!

"One old song, a thousand memories" – Anonymous

This was the day they both dreamed about, the day they believed was never going to happen. Leya sat with Aunty Reggie holding her hands in hers with Jay sitting across them as Aunty Reggie began her story. "We were hopelessly in love with each other. Neither of our families liked the idea of us together. For starters, he was a Hausa boy and 15 years older, my Musti as I called him. Mustapha and I would sneak out to meet each other, hanging out until dawn sometimes and sneaking back home. Most times I'd get home to my parents waiting for me with a cane ready to design my body" she smiled. "Still, this did not deter me nor him from seeing each other. Some called it infatuation and assured our parents, we were going to get over it. One day, one thing led to another and we did it." Jay smiled, bowing his head slightly embarrassed. "We decided we were going to get married, so it did not matter anyway. After that, we would meet anytime we could, to spend time together in every sense of that word. One day, I fell ill, mama took me to the doctor. Doctor looked at my mother and said Mrs Okafor, this is not illness now. Your daughter is 10 weeks pregnant, my mother almost collapsed. My parents were so disappointed in me. They had huge plans for me as I was very intelligent and had scholarships already lined up. Even then, Musti would not leave. He was determined to marry me so we could raise our baby. My parents fumed at the disrespect. How could Musti and his family? When I had a bright future ahead of me." Aunty Reggie began to cough and hold her chest, Leya got up to go get her some water. "Thank you. My baby!" Aunty Reggie smiled at Leya who handed her the glass of water and sat back next to her, holding her hand as she continued. "Musti and I were willing to elope, start our life somewhere. Little did I know my parents also had me on lock and key" she laughed. "They had planned to give my baby away after birth and then get the scholarship sorted as soon as possible so I move away. Went through all 9 months of pregnancy with Mustapha never abandoning me. He would steal his way into our home at midnight, scaling the wall and holding me in his arms, singing to you sometimes" she looked at Leya. "Even though he had the croakiest voice ever, which he never admitted to." Jay and Leya giggled. Aunty Reggie continued, "One night, I started to feel terrible abdominal pains. I didn't know then, it was my contractions setting in. I shouted to my mother who came in and then she shouted for my dad. My dad entered, took one look at me and then at my mum and all he said was, *"It's time. Call Mr and Mrs Bassey."* "Hours later, you were born." Aunty Reggie said looking at Leya and smiling. "You were so tiny and beautiful, still so beautiful. I got attached to you from the moment I held you in my arms. Second night after your birth, I heard my parents arguing. My mother had fallen in love with you and I could hear my mother saying *"I can take care of the baby whilst she goes back to school"* and my dad shouting *"No, no. This was not the agreement. Besides the Basseys are already coming for the baby."* My heart sunk! Who was coming for my child? No! No one was taking you away from me. So that night, I decided to hide you. I had it all planned out. I was going to run away, place you in an orphanage, look for a job nearby and when I was financially stable, I would come for you and we will live together forever." "Did you tell Mustapha?" Jay asked. "Yes, yes I did. He agreed to the plan even though he wanted me to run away with him to his other family in Kano. However, I didn't like the idea of being totally dependent on him and his family. It was Musti's idea that we mark you with the same unique inscription under my arm in case you got mixed up with the other babies. The night we marked you, you cried! Oh my, you cried. Unfortunately, the Basseys came a day earlier than my planned date. That was the most painful day of my life, worst day ever! You were forcefully taken away from me amidst my screams. I pleaded with my father, dragging my mother's dress to stop them but she felt so helpless. All hope lost, I asked for just one favour, they all turned to look at me as I asked that they call you Fa'izah, because your father loved that name and I called you Ifedimma meaning something good. I placed a locket your father had given me around your little neck as I watched you leave. A part of me died the day you were taken" tears fell from Aunty Reggie's eyes as Leya wiped them with her hand before wiping her own eyes. "How did I end up in an orphanage then?" Leya asked. "6 months later, my parents got word that the Basseys had split up and none of them wanted the responsibility of keeping a child that was not theirs." ".....they could have just brought the baby back to your parents surely?" Jay asked almost in anger. Aunty Reggie sighed,

"Unfortunately we had moved away from the North 3 weeks after giving you up. According to my father, to wipe any memories of Mustapha or you" she said looking at Leya. "As fate would have it, Musti and I met again 10 years later" she laughed. "Here he was, still looking hot as ever. Boy was hot like fire" Leya and Jay giggled. "It was like we were never apart and the first thing he asked about, was you." I explained I had been looking for you for years to no avail. I tried to find you initially, when I heard the Basseys had also moved to another state when you were taken from me. Obviously to start a new life and pretend you were theirs. I cut ties with my father for what he did to me, the pain of neglecting his own grandchild broke me and it took me a very long time to forgive him. My mother helped to look for you, she searched everywhere. One day, mama went for a church convention and met the former Mrs Bassey who was also in attendance. She told mama that in her frustration, she left you in front of an orphanage and did not make note of the name of the setting. Mama asked her to show us the orphanage, at least take us there so we could get you back. This woman kept giving excuses and that is how we never saw her again." "So you married my father?" Leya asked. "Oh yes" Aunty Reggie smiled "Yes, my

Musti. We married, travelled the world all still trying to have kids. Oh the many nights I cried feeling it was God's way of punishing me for abandoning you. Musti would hold me in his arms and comfort me. We tried everything which failed and I could not bear the thought of adopting a child when my own was out there somewhere. I prayed to God every night that if you were alive, my only wish was to meet you, even if it was on my dying day. And here you are, the girl I took into my home, into my arms, under my wings was my very own child. My Fa'izah! I wish your father was here to see this day." Leya excused herself to her room as Aunty Reggie and Jay looked at her bewildered. Within minutes, she returned holding a beautiful oval shaped turquoise locket. The one thing she had always held on to, and protected with her life. "Here is your locket. A gift from the love of your life. It has travelled with me, experienced many painful journeys along the way, but still found itself back to its rightful owner." Aunty Reggie stood up, hugging Leya in tears before leading her to the framed picture of Musti. She lit a candle as Leya did the same, "Baby, our girl is home" Aunty Reggie said smiling, her face covered in tears. Jay wrapped his arms around Leya as they looked on.

"To describe my mother would be to write about a hurricane in its perfect power. Or the climbing falling colors of a rainbow"- Maya Angelou

20

"Rise above the storm and you will find the sunshine" –
Mario Fernandez

The night before had been the most magical experience ever!
Jay had gone back to the hotel after the chance revelation
between Leya and Aunty Reggie. The bitter sweet story that
ensued and the various emotions that over powered the room, it
was simply magical. Leya had found her birth mum! It felt so
unreal, a moment so surreal, Jay could still not believe as he
relayed the night's events to his cousin Fred. "Nooo way" Fred
exclaimed in shock. "Yes way man, like, it has been the most
eventful travel of my life" Jay chuckled. "From finding Leya to
finding out the woman she works for and lives with, is her real
mum. Dude, sick!" Fred laughed, "Wow! How's Leya by the

way?" He asked. "She's doing great, still as beautiful as ever. Man, that girl blows my mind. All the time" Jay smiled at the thought of Leya. "Oh, I know that, we all do. Dami still there?" Fred enquired. Jay looked towards the bathroom "Yeah she is." "You're going to tell her?" Fred asked. "Yup" Jay sighed. "Well, let me know if you require an ambulance after the talk" Fred joked. Jay laughed, "Not sure Dami is the type but then again, you never know. Be on stand by for any emergencies." They both laughed as Jay hung up. Dami walked out of the bathroom towards Jay, "I heard my name" she smiled seductively. "Yeah that was Fred." "Oh Fred! Hope he's okay. Anyways…" she said wrapping her arms around Jay's neck, "It's been days since I've been here. You've been so busy. I mean, we haven't even really kissed each other or gotten close. Do you not miss me babe?" she asked coyly, looking towards the bed. Jay took her arms away from his neck, his face pensive, "Dami, we need to talk……"

"Life takes you to unexpected places. Love brings you home" – Melissa McClone

Finding her birth mom was the beginning of a whole new dimension to Leya's identity. Jay had arranged a private jet for

Leya and Aunty Reggie to go back home. They had insisted he came along with them but he rejected their offer as this was a journey of discovery and the ultimate intimate moments to be shared between a mother and her child. There was a lot of catching up to do!

Arriving at the large loud airport, she felt nervous. The smell of traveler suitcases hovered around, some passengers scurried past her whilst some slowly dragged their feet and luggage, enjoying the sights whilst waiting to board their flights. The sight of airplanes ready for boarding gave her mixed emotions. Leya had never been in an airplane and her first time had been filled with anxiety. She was not sure whether to be scared or excited. Nervous? Definitely! The Jet was a true luxury home in the sky, the conceptual interior of this jet beautifully portrayed elements one may find in a home and looked more like an expensive hotel suite. Leya pulled the warm blanket over her body as she shivered at the cool air coming through the vents. As the plane took off the runway, shaking ferociously, she held on to her mother's hand – her mother! She loved calling her that! Looking out the small oval shaped window, she was overcome with the magnificent feeling of being on top of the world.

****

Holding hands, the first stop was at the Okafor's home in Eastern Nigeria and Aunty Reggie's grip tightened as she took one look at the home she grew in, the streets she walked on and the home that brought beautiful and painful memories. It felt weird being home after a long time away. Her mum had always visited her in Abuja as Aunty Reggie could not bear coming home to see her father. Nothing much had changed except for a few cracks on the wall, the faded grey paint on the building and the withered guava trees in the compound. She smiled with nostalgia written all over her face. Leya lay her head on her mother's shoulder reassuringly as they walked through the gates. Aunty Reggie raised her hand to knock on the door, she hesitated, taking deep breaths. Suddenly, they heard a sound coming from inside, like strong loud strides. The door opened and a grey haired woman in her mid seventies embraced her in a warm tight hug! She looked over at Leya, her eyes filled with love but wide in shock surprise. "Fa'izah?" she asked, her voice faint but audible. Before Aunty Reggie and Leya could confirm her question, she enveloped Leya in her arms, "Welcome home" she said, kissing her on the cheek! Were it not for the lines on her grandmother's face, grey hair held neatly in a bun and some loose skin, Leya would have thought Mrs Okafor was a decade younger. Her speech was articulate and she had the charm of a youth, her movement as agile as a monkey and her heart was tender and kind natured. In each smile she was a queen, her words flowed with wisdom. Leya had imagined what she would have looked like as a young lady as they spent the hours talking, laughing, and occasionally breaking down in tears. Each speech further expatiating her genealogical history and the family she came from. It felt surreal!

They had made the painful visit to the burial place of her grandfather, whose tombstone she had stared at in sober reflection, a million questions running through her mind. Leya had decided, just as her mum did in the weeks before his death, that the greatest gift she could give herself was forgiveness. For in forgiveness, she was freeing herself from the pain and no longer a prisoner to it. Leaving some beautiful scented white calla lilies and orchid flowers over her grandfather's grave as a sign of peace offering, they had gone on to make the journey to visit Musti's family home in Zaria. The home had high walls and a black ornate double gate curved at the top. It was a large house situated in the quiet area of G.R.A and once again, Leya was filled with nervous anticipation and Aunty Reggie an almost childlike excitement. She had always gotten on with Jamilah, Musti's younger sister who had been overjoyed to hear the good news about finding Leya. As the gates opened automatically and the car drove through, Leya held her mother's hand. Her heart pounding and almost breaking into a sweat, here she was, about to meet her other family. A desire she had longed for, for many years! Aunty Reggie glanced at her daughter and smiled warmly. Standing at the huge glazed oak door of the house was a very beautiful lady, wearing a white luxurious floor length kaftan with an ornate embellished design of gold beads, shimmering sequins and crystals. Jamilah rushed to hug Aunty Reggie as Leya looked on, playing with her fingers. "Reginaaaa" Jamilah screamed exhilarated. "I missed you." "I missed you more Jamilah, at least thanks to technology, we speak all the time?" Aunty Reggie said to her. "Speaking is different from seeing each other abeg. Ah, ah…" she said, turning to look at Leya. "Fa'izah! Allahu Akbar!" Jamilah exclaimed, thrilled as she went over to embrace Leya. "You are home baby girl, come, come in, you need to meet your family" excitedly holding Leya's hands into the large living area.

She looked around in awe – it was a beautiful family home with gold plated ornate furniture and framed pictures of family members including one with Aunty Reggie and her father. The home screamed of royalty and this explained Leya's perception of her aunty Jamilah who was not only one of the most beautiful women she had ever seen but she possessed grace as a swan! Indeed her name Jamilah was a true reflection of the woman who stood before her. Something about her radiated from within and seeing her, Leya understood what her mother meant when she would always say to her from the moment she met her at Aunty Tina's fabric shop – that she bore a striking resemblance to someone she knew. Looking at Aunty Jamilah was as Leya looking in the mirror and seeing a reflection of herself – her older self. Jamilah had introduced Leya to her two female cousins who were just as thrilled to meet her as Jamilah was. She had been informed about her other cousins, 2 males and a female, who lived all over the globe in various continents. As they got to know each other, the little kids ran up to her, grabbing her hand, wanting to be close to her as she bent down to hug them warmly. Video calls had been made to her cousins outside the country who could not wrap their heads around how much Leya looked like their mother. The moments had been filled with strong emotions of tears and lots of laughter as they all finally settled on the floor cross legged. The cook served the most delicious Tuwon chinkafah *rice balls* and miyan kuka *baobab leaves soup*. With their hands dipping in and out of the meal and the youngest niece on Leya's lap, their warmth was just what she'd hoped for and meeting her birth family had strengthened the bond they all shared.

****

The trip of discovery was all Leya needed and as they returned to Abuja after a week in Zaria, her heart was full! The journey had compensated for all the wrongs in her life and she chuckled at the thought of her mannerisms that was clearly from her Dad's side of the family. She and her mum had visited her father's grave often, spending time engaging in conversations with him as though he were with them. Leaving her grandmother had been overwhelming, she had fallen in love with Chinyere Okafor. Leya had tried to convince her to come along with them but she had gently declined chuckling that she was no longer used to city life. It was hard leaving her behind after the beautiful moments they shared, staying up late and laughing into the early hours of the night, taking long lazy walks and generally enjoying each other's company. *What an amazing bond they would have shared if her Grandfather had kept her,* Leya thought to herself. Leya was comforted with the fact that Chi girl as she had fondly started calling her, was surrounded by love and people who genuinely cared and provided for her. It had been an emotional journey back home, a journey that answered a lot of questions and filled the void that lay within her for many years. Aunty Jamilah had sternly but lovingly instructed her to visit home often which she gladly obliged to. Back home, as they perused old pictures of her mum and dad with Aunty Reggie's arms around her, they chuckled at the photographic memories. "Hah! Look at the locket on you when you were a teenager" Leya said smiling. "My goodness, daddy was so handsome" she continued. Aunty Reggie laughed, "It's a really strange world. Can you imagine? All these while and my own daughter lived under the same roof as I and I didn't even know." "…and you treated me so well" Leya said hugging her. She glanced at Aunty Reggie and said almost in a childlike tone, "My mummy!" and hugged her again. "My heart is so full." Aunty Reggie said breathing a sigh of relief, her eyes closed. "I see the way Jay looks at you, just the way your father used to look at me" Aunty Reggie mentioned, her gaze fixed on a picture of Mustapha. "Ehnn but daddy didn't used to give you unnecessary wahala like mine" Leya rolled her eyes. Aunty Reggie laughed, "Young love" she said, before breaking down in a hysterical cough. "You need to see a doctor mummy, this cough is not going away" Leya said worryingly. "I knowww" Aunty Reggie stressed amidst more deep coughs. "Let me get you some water" Leya said, rushing to the kitchen and pouring some water in a cup. She returned to see Aunty Reggie sprawled on the floor unconscious. Leya screamed, dropping the cup and running towards her, "Mummy, mummy!" she shouted.

"The greatest healing therapy is friendship and love" – Hubert Humphrey

Jay arrived at the hospital ward holding Leya in his arms comforting her. He had flown back to Abuja after they returned from their "homecoming" trip and had been thrilled at all the stories Leya and Aunty Reggie told him. The glee in her eyes made his heart so warm, this was the Leya he knew. His body longed for her and he could not wait to have her all to himself.

Barely relaxed back at the hotel, he had gotten the frantic call from Leya. "I rushed here immediately. How is she?" He asked, a look of worry on his face as he turned to look at Aunty Reggie lying on the bed, her eyes closed, an intravenous infusion inserted into her vein. "She seems okay" Leya looked at her mum as Jay stroked her arm gently. The doctor walked in and went over to Aunty Reggie, checking the drip and her pulse. Every move he made was calculating and purposeful. His posture stiff, he turned to Jay and Leya, "Hello, my name is Doctor Roberts" he smiled. His eyes cold and distant as most doctors, he continued, "May I have a word with you two please" leading them to his office. Anxiously sitting down, he sighed, "Mrs Hussein's cancer is..." "Cancer!" Leya shouted, almost jumping out her chair in anguish, Jay calmed her down. "Yes, she's at stage 4 Ovarian cancer, there's not much we can do for her now" he continued. Leya covered her mouth with her hands stifling her tears. "How is this at stage 4 already" Jay asked, his left hand holding Leya's. "She was diagnosed a year ago but she refused chemo or any form of treatment. She said she was ready to go join her husband and in the moments she had, she just wanted to live" Doctor Roberts continued. "I can't lose her" Leya said in

242

tears looking at Jay, "I can't." Jay held her hand firmly. Doctor Roberts sighed again, this time, his eyes were filled with sadness. "I didn't realise she had a daughter until recently when she called me extremely excited and wanting to know if she could start some form of chemo, but it was already too late. The cancer had spread to other parts of her body forming secondary cancers. It is likely to continue to spread which can lead to respiratory failure or even heart failure. I'm really sorry" he said getting up. Patting Leya's shoulder gently, he walked out leaving the two of them to process the information. How could this happen? Leya, overcome with grief put her head in her hands as Jay looked on helplessly, rubbing her back. He had spent the rest of the time in Doctor Robert's office holding Leya, his hands gently caressing her as she buried her face in his chest, when the nurse came round to notify them Aunty Reggie was awake. "Why didn't you tell me mummy?" Leya asked, lines of dried tears on her face as she sat next to her mum on the bed, holding her hand. "And mess up the beautiful moments I'd had with you even before finding out you were my daughter? No oh! Knowing you, you would have babied me to insanity." Leya forced a sad smile. "Cheer up" Aunty Reggie lifted Leya's chin up. "I can't lose you mummy,

243

not now, not when I've finally found you" Leya said, her voice hushed. Jay walked over to put his hands on her shoulder. Aunty Reggie looked at both of them, "You two remind me so much of my baby boy and I. My Musti of life" She said smiling. "He loved me against all odds." She asked for both their hands and as they stretched out their hands to her, she placed hers on theirs. "My baby girl and her handsome fella. I always prayed to God to meet my daughter again, even if it was just for one day or on my death bed. Instead he gave me over a year filled with beautiful memories with you. This God is too good" she said briefly looking up the ceiling. "Not only did I meet you, I met Jay too. I've even witnessed your lover's quarrel" she teased. "I'll always be around you two, always. If you ever feel a soft wind around either of you, it would only be me just passing by to say heyyyy." They laughed, albeit pensive. Leya pulled her hand away, "Stop talking like you're leaving us because you're not going anywhere." "Ah! So as you two are head over heels in love with each other, you don't want me to go and also enjoy my man abi?" Aunty Reggie asked chuckling. "Not just yet." Jay cut in. "You have many more memories to share with this beauty right here and some grandkids maybe?" He said, gazing warmly at Leya.

"Unfortunately, I have to be back in Lagos tonight for an emergency board meeting and some wrap up sessions. I'll be back as soon as possible and you Aunty Reggie, will be here to welcome me with a waltz" he looked at Aunty Reggie affectionately. "Ahhh, I can't wait" she said. Jay put his hands on Leya's shoulders as she stood up from the bed. "I'll be back" he whispered to her. "Stay strong for her. I love you, very much." His beautiful eyes staring into hers for a brief moment, before arching his head to kiss her softly on her lips and on her forehead. Aunty Reggie looked on blushing. "I'll see you ladies soon" he smiled, before walking out.

"Remember the joy, the laughter, the smiles. I've only gone to rest a while" – Anonymous

Jay had constantly checked on Aunty Reggie and Leya on his return to Lagos. She was doing well but still in hospital being monitored. He could not bear to think how distraught Leya would be if anything happened to her mother. It had taken her 28 years to meet her birth mom and she had been so elated that her happiness radiated from within. He was in the office with Fred, Mike Suleiman, Priscilla and other staff members discussing the agenda when his phone rang. He answered the call and rushed out the door leaving the others stunned and confused by his action. Jay had immediately taken a private jet and arrived at the hospital as quickly as he could. Running into the building, he stopped in his tracks when he saw Leya in the hallway. Her eyes were swollen from the tears she had cried, he knew! Jay's heart broke seeing her in such despair. As grief surged within her, she looked at him nodding her head sideways to confirm what he already knew. Jay watched her slowly descend to the ground and ran to catch her, holding her in his arms as they both descended on to the floor together. Leya wailed!

Aunty Reggie's funeral had been well attended and the service was beautiful. It went on to prove how loved she was by all. Leya had never experienced heart wrenching grief as she did when her mother's casket was being lowered into the ground. Her mother! She had felt an emptiness only a mother's warmth could fill, and as the salty tears flowed freely from her eyes, she smiled briefly at the memories they made which played like a beautiful song in her head. Her mother was gone, sleeping peacefully next to her father, reunited in love once again. Looking on one more time as the grave was being covered, Leya put her arm through her grandma Chi girl's arm as they looked at each other nodding without saying a word and walking away. Jay and Fred had become the hosts at Aunty Reggie's house where they had gathered for a small reception. They shook hands with the guests who offered their condolence before they left and ensured everything was going smoothly. Her grandma had left right after the funeral even with Leya's persistence on wanting her to stay. "You're all I have now Ifedimma. I'll come visit very soon and spend all the time you want us to. For now, let me grieve my baby alone" she had said smiling and kissing Leya on the cheek before leaving. Aunty Jamilah walked over to Leya sitting quietly on the sofa. She took her hand in hers, patting it. "You know I'll always be here for you if you need me. Zaria is your home." Leya looked at her older reflection and nodded. Aunty Jamilah smiled, "I see you have yourself a good man over there" she looked over at Jay. Leya let out a shy smile, "You have to bring him home sometime" Aunty Jamilah continued. "I will" Leya responded, her voice faint. Aunty Jamilah hugged her warmly, "See you soon Fa'izah. Allah ya ba ki karfi" she said, asking God to give Leya strength in Hausa. Getting up to leave, Aunty Jamilah walked over to Jay, engaging in a short conversation before hugging him and walking out the door. Jay occasionally turned to look over at Leya whilst still speaking with guests at the door. Aunty Tina walked over to Leya, sitting down and putting her arm around her, "I'm so sorry Fa'izah." Stunned, Leya looked up at Aunty Tina who gave her a knowing smile. "Your mum told me the beautiful news when she found out. She was so happy. My dear friend's prayer everyday was to see her daughter again even if it was her last day on earth. However, God gave you two a much longer time together." "She was an amazing woman" Leya uttered. "I know, I knew her for 18 years. She and your father! One of the best friends I ever had and the best couple I'd ever known. Their love radiated from within" Aunty Tina replied. Leya smiled and looked at the picture of her mum and dad in a frame side by side on the console table. "Listen, I'm leaving back to Ghana but if you ever need anything, anything at all. Call me, you have my number." Leya nodded and responded, "Thank you Aunty T. For everything. God placed you at the right time and the right place for you to find me. In that, I found my true self." Aunty Tina hugged her, tears in her eyes and then stood up to leave. She stopped briefly by the picture of Aunty Reggie and her husband, smiled and walked away.

Chioma had been busy serving the guests and instructing the other girls from the Bistro, ensuring the atmosphere was what Aunty Reggie would have wanted. She walked over to Leya with a tray of drinks. "Do you want anything to eat or drink?" Leya nodded her head. "Leya now, you have to drink something. Even if you won't eat, at least drink something" she said worryingly. Fred approached them, "What's wrong?" he asked. "This girl wants to kill herself o, doesn't want to eat, doesn't want to drink" Chioma responded. Fred took a deep breath sighing and sat next to her. "Leya, or would you like me to call you Fa'izah or Ifedimma?" He nudged her, making her smile. "If anything, your mum wouldn't have loved seeing you this way. So what do you say we raise a toast to an awesome lady?" He took two glasses from Chioma's tray, handing one to Leya. "To Aunty Reggie" Fred said, clicking his glass with Leya's as they both took a sip. Jay, still standing by the door, watched Leya and Fred, his heart was content!

"Intimacy is not purely physical. It is the act of connecting with someone so deeply, you feel like you can see into their soul" – Anonymous

249

It was night time and everyone had left. The room awfully silent as the crickets began to sing the night away. Leya sat cross legged quietly on the sofa with Jay beside her. "Fred?" She asked. "He had to fly back to Lagos tonight" Jay responded, she nodded quietly. "Are you okay? Do you want me to leave? I can come....." "No! No" Leya cut in, looking at him "Don't leave. Please, stay with me" Jay moved his face closer to her, even in her despair, he could smell the alluring fruity fragrance of her body. He gazed at her, their eyes locked. "Are you sure?" His voice low and husky, she nodded again. Slowly, he moved his lips to touch hers as she closed her eyes, opening her mouth slightly as Jay slipped his tongue into it. Leya responded to his kiss, her tongue playing with his as he continued to kiss her. They pulled apart for a few seconds, their breaths shaky. They stared at each other intently and a sudden rush of emotions flooded through them, over powering their senses as they began to kiss passionately as though they were the air that filled each other's lungs. Running her hands all over his body and feeling every crevice along his perfect physique, they frantically took each other's clothes off, ripping at them. Jay arched her back on to the sofa, his hands exploring every inch of her body. Leya's breath quickened in anticipation, raising her legs slightly as Jay pulled her pant off, kissing her thighs up to the core of her woman. She gasped! He placed her hands above her head as he continued kissing all over her naked body, tracing his tongue around her hard nipples. She rolled him over and lay on top of his firm body, running her tongue up his neck and planting an intense kiss on his lips. Feeling his hardness pressed against her crotch, she moved down to take him in her mouth. "Leya" he groaned, letting out a soft moan in ecstasy. Moments later, she straddled him as they became one, her soft supple breast pressed against his hard muscular chest, he cupped them, gently taking them in his mouth as their bodies continued to dance in tune with one another, electrified at each other's sensual touch.

They made love until the early hours of the morning. Their love making had been wild and passionate and other times slow and gentle, swirled in all sorts of emotion. Jay and Leya spooned naked on the living room floor lost in thought, their clothes strewn all over. He stroked her arm, idly tracing his fingers up and down as they held each other. "Come with me to Lagos" he said to her. She turned to face him, "I can't Jay, and I cannot just walk out and leave mummy's business. She worked too hard to have this closed down" Leya replied. "Who said anything about leaving the business or closing it down? I have businesses all over the country, I don't have to be in one particular place to ensure its working? I mean, you hire competent people to do the job. Besides Chioma seems responsible enough to manage it." Leya turned back to her original position, her back fitting into the curves of Jay's body. "Lagos is not for me. Besides, it's not like your family is accepting of me anyways." "Would Fred be here for the funeral if he didn't accept you?" Jay asked. Leya sighed, "Okay Fred yes, but your mum" she said getting up from the floor. She caught Jay's gaze, "What are you looking at?" she asked, a playful frown on her face as she picked up his shirt from the floor and wore it. "You! All of you" he responded, watching admiringly as she tried to close the buttons which had not been ripped from their frantic love making. "Damn, you're beautiful, and that booty" Jay teased. "Yeye man!" Leya smiled, throwing a cushion at him. She loved the way he loved her, the way he always looked at her. Amidst the pain of losing her mother, she found pleasure with him. "Where're you going?" Jay asked as Leya walked towards the kitchen. "Going to get a drink," she replied. Even with her back facing him, she could feel his gaze on her, she smiled. Jay watched her leave, her hips swaying in the oversized shirt, its sleeves longer than her arms. There was something about her wearing his shirt which he found seductive. A look of satisfaction on his face, he got up, putting on his boxers as Leya entered a few minutes later with two glasses of juice. He sat on the sofa taking a sip before placing the glass on the table, "...as I was saying, we can open many more Aunty Reggie's Bistro all over the country in her honour. Chioma can run this branch." "You don't understand or you're just pretending not to. I am also a few weeks to graduating from school here." "You can always come back to graduate," He remarked. "Jay! I'm not going back to Lagos, that's your base and people know you. Do you want everyone around to keep reminding you of who I was?" She asked, her voice raised. "Who cares what they think?" He asked. "You do!" Leya exclaimed, picking up her clothes from the floor. "You succumbed to pressure the last time and hurt me. And you want me to come back and go through that again?" She stopped to look at him, the clothes in her hands, he was quiet. "Say something Jay, answer me. Look at my hand, look" putting her scarred hand towards his face "This! This is the scar from that night." Jay held her hand and slowly took the scar to his lips, kissing it. She pulled back, "No Jay, not now" as she placed the clothes in the chair. "So what are you saying?" He asked. "I'm saying that I'm staying here and minding my business." "What about me? What about us? Dami is gone, well, not without the slap I received when I told her about you. What more do you want?" "What do I want Jay?" Leya asked. "YES, what? I have shown you time and again how much I love you." He rubbed his head in frustration. "Well, your mother once said love was not enough" Leya reminded him. He walked over, cupping her face in his hands and looking into her eyes, "I want a life with you, to travel the world with you. I want to have babies with you. I want to grow old and grey with you Leya Ifedimma Fa'izah Hussein." Raising her hand, she stroked his face lovingly, "Oh Jay!" before moving away from his grip. "After everything I've said, you're still not convinced. What do you want me to do Leya? Cut my head before you realise how much I want you?" His voice raised. "So why are you shouting?" she asked, her feistiness coming out to play. "I'm not shouting" Jay said exasperated "Yes you are" Leya retorted. Suddenly, they were silent and Jay sat down. Staring at the man she loved with all her heart, she walked over to him, lifted his hand from his thigh and sat on his lap facing him. Her arms wrapped around his neck, he looked the other way ignoring her. Leya turned Jay's head back to look at her. As they stared at each other in utter silence, they burst out laughing before Leya pressed her lips against his, kissing him. He responded, eyes closed, savouring every taste of her lips on his. "I lost you once, I'm not about to lose you again" he murmured.

"You can't go back and change the beginning, but you can start where you are and change the ending" – C.S Lewis

Aunty Reggie's Bistro was back in business following its shut down for the funeral and an extra few days of mourning. Customers came and went as usual and Leya was sorting out the menu of the day board with Chioma when Elena walked in. With Leya's back facing the customer whose presence she could feel, she apologised, "Please bear with me, I'll be with you in a....." She froze, looking at Elena in shock. "Hi Leya" Elena said smiling, "Ermm, hel, hello" Leya replied nervously. "Can I have a few minutes of your time seeing you're quite busy at the moment?" Elena asked. She looked just as Leya remembered and in a way, her poise and elegance reminded her of her Aunty Jamilah. A realisation hit her! If she looked exactly like Aunty

Jamilah, then indeed, she too did possess that aura of elegance and needed to hold herself in high esteem. After all, once queen of the night, always a queen! Smiling at the thought, she responded confidently, "Yes, sure" as she motioned Chioma to take over and gestured Elena towards a seat. Elena sat down, looking around "Nice place you have here." she admired. "I'm so sorry about your mother" she continued. Leya nodded, "Thank you." "Well, I came to visit the project site and thought to pass by first and offer my condolence. Also, to speak to you about my son." Leya shifted uncomfortably! Why was she uncomfortable? Was she not a queen? "When you left the last time, I saw what it did to him. Gbenga loves you, he has proven beyond every reasonable doubt how you keep him going, wanting to be the best version of himself. Might I add that I am extremely proud to see how well you're doing? School, taking over your mum's business and doing an amazing job at it I hear…." Elena placed her perfectly manicured fingers on Leya's hand, which stunned her. "My darling, relationships hardly thrive when two people live miles apart. I'll leave you to ponder on that" She got up. "Besides, I love having him come for the family barbecue and only your magic does it. Now, unfortunately, I must be on my way." She looked around at the mouth-watering pictures of the food available, Elena said to Leya, "The pictures of the menu look so appetising, maybe another time, I'll try a dish." She picked up her graphite coloured ostrich Hermes Birkin bag and headed towards the door. Stopping at the exit, she turned to look at Leya, "You're still as beautiful as the first day I met you." Elena smiled and walked out leaving Leya's mouth slightly ajar.

"There are only two times I want to be with you: Now and Forever" - Anonymous

Jay missed Leya and each time they spoke, he always tried to convince her to move over! He understood her loyalty towards Aunty Reggie's Bistro. Who wouldn't? It belonged to her mother and she intended to make sure it was as successful as when Aunty Reggie was alive. They spoke every day and although he could not touch her as he desired, he loved seeing her face via their many video calls. He had spoken to her a few hours before and decided to catch up on what was going round the world on television. As he sat on his sofa topless with a blanket wrapped around him, he heard the doorbell ring. He checked the time on the wall clock, *"Who could this be?"* he thought, before getting up reluctantly to go open the door.

In shocked expression, he stared at her. "Are you going to say something or we are just going to stand here and look at each other" Leya said smiling. Jay continued to look at her dumbfounded, she was here! "Ah, ah! Say something now. Why are you acting like you've seen a ghost!" He pinched her arm playfully and she shrieked. "What was that for?" She asked wincing in pain. "You're not a ghost then" he said, a small smile playing on his lips. Quietly, he gazed at her, enjoying the moment. The look that always made her knees tremble, "You came back!" He said. "Yes, and next time I'm travelling, you're booking me on a private jet. All these yeye road journeys can frustrate someone ehnn. We stopped at..." Jay grabbed her face and kissed her before she could finish. He carried her, wrapping the blanket around both of them. His forehead pressed against hers as she wrapped her arms around him, he asked, "You're here to stay?" "Yesssss" she whispered. He smiled, "Welcome home Mrs Daniels!"

EPILOGUE

"These people will not kill me o! Ani, wo' ni kpa mi." Bunmi shouted, repeating her words in Yoruba. "Ah, ah! Kilode? What is it?" She echoed in English. "Where is Baba Saliu's soup? Do you want him to swallow his Amala with water?" Bunmi yelled at one of her staff who was nervously gathering a bowl to plate the customer's soup. "Sorry ma!" the girl apologised. "Sorry for yourself!" Bunmi retorted angrily. A dark grey Porsche had just arrived, parking by the Buka. Curiously, Bunmi turned her head to the side to look. *"Ah, ah! Bunmi, see your level o, Porsche keh? To your Buka?"* She muttered under her breath smiling. Still looking, the plates in her hands dropped to the floor crashing in a million pieces as she ran to embrace Leya. Her tears flowed uncontrollably. It had been forever and a day since they last saw or spoke to each other. Bunmi could not control her emotions as she let out a heartfelt cry her speech was incoherent. Tears of joy! Her Leya baby was back and she looked so good in her thin strap, extra wide leg, satin African print jumpsuit. Her hair was in a messy high bun as usual with large hoop ear rings. Bunmi stopped to look at Leya, turning her around before hugging her again and bursting into fits of laughter. Her emotions were all over the place, she could not believe her Leya was right there before her. Assessing Leya up and down, Bunmi spotted the emerald cut, light pink diamond ring on her left finger. "Leya baabyyyyy" she shouted gleefully, bouncing up and down on Leya. Jay laughed so hard his shoulders trembled. Calming herself down, she looked at Jay and then at Leya, shaking her head at both of them with a smile before leading them into her Buka. There was so much to talk about!

The End

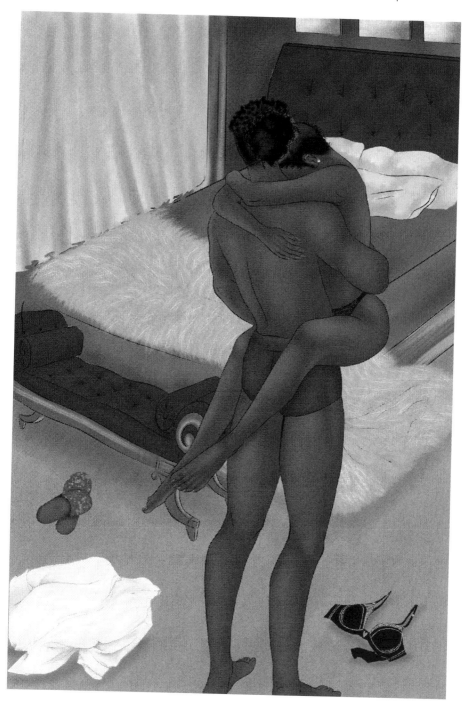

RE1Masstecmedia COMBO 4

Greedier - Soocialmedia

Pass: Socialmedia@2020

Printed in Poland
by Amazon Fulfillment
Poland Sp. z o.o., Wrocław

59846412R00150